Under the
Pawpaw
Trees

Cheryl King

Purple Marble Press

Texas

Published by Purple Marble Press

Copyright © 2023 by Cheryl King

ISBN:

Paperback: 978-1-7377858-3-5

Ebook: 978-1-7377858-4-2

Cover artwork by 100Covers

Dedication

To the people God has put in my path:
You are appreciated.

1

Vengeful Thoughts

December 1934

The first time I thought about killin' Paul, I was sittin' out under the pawpaw trees, on Josy and Daddy's graves. It was just a fleeting thought then, no real plan or nothin'. But thinkin' about everything I'd gone through put the idea of revenge in my head.

I couldn't get over losin' my brother Josy. He was more than a brother – he was the person in the world I looked up to the most. I'll never forget the day ol' Charlie and Pate brung him home all beat up by railroad bulls and barely alive. Three days. He lasted three days after they brung him home. And our world just fell apart after that.

I tried everything to take care of Mama and Daddy, 'cause those were Josy's last words, *Take care of Mama and Daddy*. I went huntin', trappin', and tradin', but nothin' was enough. We were too far behind on our mortgage, Mama was sick, Daddy couldn't do much 'cause of losin' his hand in that axe accident, and besides, both of them were plumb useless 'cause of grief.

So I followed in Josy's footsteps and hopped a train, hopin' to find work. I did find work, but I also found Paul Burnett, the railroad bull who took me offa that train and took my heart too.

Paul was big and broad shouldered but soft and gentle as a teddy bear. He wrote poetry and snuck caramel cubes into my pockets on the clothesline and smoothed aloe on my sunburnt skin and watched sunsets with me and held my hands when we danced on Fourth of July and told me I sparkled like fireworks. He made me feel things I had never felt before. I believe he introduced me to love.

And then he introduced me to the most horrible feelings I could have ever imagined. Because I found out that Paul was one of the bulls that beat up Josy.

The second time I thought about killin' Paul, I got more serious about it, started makin' a plan. I had just gotten that apology note from him, and all those memories came back in a tidal wave.

I had to go talk to Josy, rollin' our purple marble in my fingers, tryin' to block the vision of Josy in that pine box and Daddy crumpling to the ground, me puttin' our jar of marbles into the crook of Josy's arm before they closed the casket, and keepin' my favorite purple one so's I could have somethin' to remember Josy by, a token, a connection.

I was glad Paul brought my marble back – it had been a mistake to give it to him in the first place – but he's the reason Josy's in that pine box. Pate told me about it. It was Pate who witnessed the beating and Pate who recognized Paul when we went to the Burnett farm to work for the winter. So, naturally, it was Pate I thought about findin' to help me hunt Paul down and do to him exactly what he did to Josy. Except I planned to use my pistol.

Paul left me the note and the purple marble, and it was the marble that I cared about. The note, I ripped that into a million pieces and watched them float away like paper ghosts in the wind. Then I ran out to Josy's grave and cried and cried.

Josy was my hero. Boy, I idolized him – still do. He couldn't do nothin' wrong in my eyes, and that made his death all the more tragic. For me and for Mama and Daddy. And if it weren't for his death, I believe Daddy'd still be here too.

Daddy's death came so suddenly and unexpectedly. I tried to pretend it was an accident, like the one that took his hand, or that he plumb worked himself to death, or even that he got thrown from our mule, Molly, even though she couldn't throw nobody if she tried. I made up these scenarios 'cause the truth was too hard to bear. But Daddy just couldn't take Josy's death. He blamed himself. 'Course I blame Paul. For all of it. The way I see it, Paul killed Josy and Daddy. There's no gettin' around that fact.

Now, as I watch Pastor Klein, Mr. Macafee, and Mr. Clay lower a third pine box into the ground under the pawpaw trees, next to Josy and Daddy, I'm thinkin' about killin' Paul again. And this time, I mean it.

2

Grief

Grief is a lonely, miserable place. There's no one to talk to about what I'm feeling. Tons of folks in town are all the time saying *Let me know if you need anything*, but then they go back to their lives and put me in a position where I'd actually have to reach out and *ask* for help when I need it, and someone who's grievin' does not want to ask for help. So I smile and nod and squeak out, "I'm fine, thank you," all the while prayin' that someone'll see the pain in my eyes and pull me into a hug and take care of life for me.

And Jimmy – well, since we're kinda boyfriend-girlfriend, I don't want him seein' me cryin' all the time, 'cause that would surely send him runnin' away faster than a barn cat after a field mouse. So when I'm with him, I pretend like everything's great, and we laugh and have fun no matter what we're doin'. And I pray he doesn't see right through me. Pray he doesn't hear the shakiness in my laughter, a clue that it can turn into sobbing in an instant. Besides, my time with Jimmy is truthfully the only time I can forget about bein' sad for what I've lost – at least a little bit, anyway. I don't want to ruin that, no sir.

I especially cain't talk to Mama, 'cause I believe her loss is greater than mine. She lost her husband of 18 years and her only son, and most days she's hangin' on by a thread. If I share my heartbreak with her, it will only make her feel worse than she already does, and I cain't do that to her. I have to try to be strong for her. But here's the crazy thing about it all: I reckon she's thinkin' the same exact thing, so we tiptoe around the grief, pretendin' to be strong for each other, and then we go to our separate rooms and cry ourselves to sleep.

Yep, it's a lonely place, alright. Really, the only thing I look forward to anymore, other than spendin' time with Jimmy Mack, is gettin' Margaret Ann's letters. She writes me all the time and tells me about her life in Nashville, how her sisters and brothers are doin', and what all she's been up to. Her letters are always much more exciting than my letters to her. They sure do cheer me up. After Paul left his note and my bag on the porch the other day and I had a good cry, I read and reread Margaret Ann's latest letter.

Dearest June,

You're not going to believe this, but I got a job at the beauty parlor right down the road from our house! The owner is teaching me all about doing hair. Right now I'm just washing customers' hair, but soon I'll be doing haircuts. Remember when I cut your hair before you went train hopping? I'll never forget that. I'm glad you came to me for help before going on that dangerous adventure, especially since I'd been so awful to you. I truly hope you've forgiven me.

Another bit of news: Say-Lynn's got herself a boyfriend, can you believe it? My baby sister, growing up so fast. All the others seem to still be babies, always underfoot and eating all the food in the house. I'm glad we're all back together again, even though we had to move to Nashville to make it happen. My aunt and uncle live right next door, so sometimes some of us spend the night over there, and basically it's like we have two homes!

I want you to come visit sometime, okay? And I want to hear all about Jimmy. I know you two were meant to be together. Write me real soon, June.

Friends forever,

M.A.

I smooth the letter out on my desk and pull a sheet of paper and pencil from the drawer. I've been such an emotional mess the past few days that I couldn't bring myself to write to Margaret Ann. I didn't want my letter to her to be depressing.

Dear Margaret Ann,

First off, of course I believe you got a job at a beauty parlor. You're brilliant with hair! You did such a great job cutting your brothers' and sisters' hair all the time, and then of course when you cut mine, it really did look nice. You'll be running that place soon, I bet. And I do completely forgive you. I don't think I understand what you and your mama had against Pate, but I can still forgive you, and I'm thankful that you helped me and that you're still my friend, even though you live all the way in Nashville now.

Me and Mama's been able to do a lot with our

government assistance and the work program. We got an old car! I'm learning how to drive it. I can't work at the factory in Knoxville no more because of school, but Miss Glass is letting me teach all the little girls how to sew, and Jimmy's teaching the boys how to hunt. Seems to me we should switch, and I should teach the girls how to hunt! Wouldn't that be a hoot? I don't want to ruffle any feathers, I guess.

I hope I get to see you real soon. One last thing. I've been thinking some dark thoughts lately about getting back at Paul. Don't you think he oughta pay for what he done? Tell me what you think.

Love always,

June

I don't know if it's a good idea to mention that last part. She might think I'm crazy. But I fold up the note, cram it into an envelope, and head out to the post office anyway, calling hello to the chickens on my way down the drive. Mama's at work, so she's got the car.

"Hey, Molly!" I croon as I enter the mule barn. "Ready to go into town?" She chuffs her greeting and I give her some petting before bringing her out and hitching up the wagon.

I notice three strange things on my twenty-minute ride into Maynardville. I can walk it in twenty-five, so you'd think takin' the wagon would be faster, but poor Molly's gettin' older and slower. It's worth it, though, 'cause she's the sweetest ol' mule in the history of mules, and at least I can sit down for a bit, even though it is bumpy.

Anyway, the first strange thing I notice is all up and down the lane are these long wooden poles lyin' there in the grass. I don't know who put 'em there or when or what they're for, but

7

I don't like it. I like to have an answer for everything, and I don't like mysteries. So I arrive at Main Street with a scowl on my face, and that's when I see the second strange thing – a buncha trucks that I ain't seen in Maynardville before. See, a small town like this, everybody knows everybody, and we know everybody's cars and wagons and animals. There are three big trucks parked on Main Street outside the courthouse, and they don't look like normal trucks, either.

It used to be that whenever I seen somethin' strange and wanted answers, I'd pop into Macafee's and ask him, but since Mr. Macafee closed his store down, I've had to find other folks to ask, and no offense, but most people ain't as smart or as nice as Mr. Macafee.

Mr. Clay at the feed store don't do much but grunt and nod these days, and Pastor Klein's too busy with church business to ask him anything. Miss Jane, who used to work at the Sweet Shop 'fore it closed down, well, she works at the Piggly Wiggly now, and she never knows anything 'bout what's going on. And Mrs. Linder, the biggest gossip in all of Union County, now, you'd think she'd be able to answer any question I ever had, but she's a funny one – she loves to spill secrets when no one's askin', but soon as you ask somethin', she clams up.

If I'm lucky, I'll run into Mr. Macafee in town, but today, no such luck, which is strange, and here's the third strange thing: Downtown Maynardville is downright burstin' at the seams with people bustlin' about all excited-like. With all these people runnin' 'round actin' like they got all kindsa shoppin' to do, you'd think I'd see Mr. Macafee among 'em.

I decide to ask old Mr. Willis at the post office, even though he always looks at me like he don't remember who I am, which is silly because I come into the post office near-'bout once a week.

"Hi, Mr. Willis," I say as cheerfully as I can manage, and I hand him my letter for Margaret Ann and three pennies. He takes it and nods, but there's no smile – just squinted eyes peeping out underneath a furrowed brow of bushy white caterpillars.

"Anything else I can do for you, Missy?" I wonder if he calls me "Missy" 'cause he cain't remember my name.

"No, thank you, but I do have a question." When he doesn't say anything, I go on. "What's all them big wooden poles layin' on the ground all up and down the road?"

Mr. Willis's bushy white caterpillars jump up to his receding hairline, and he acts like he might fall right off his stool. "What's all them big poles?!" he squeals. "Missy, ain't you heard? We're gettin' 'lectricity out here!"

"Electricity? What d'ya mean?"

And his eyes go big again. "What do ya mean, what do I mean? We're gettin' electricity. The president done made a law or somethin' that will get electricity strung up to the rural towns, and even the farms."

I gasp. "Even the farms? Like even my farm?" This is just about the most excitin' thing I've heard in I-don't-know-how-long.

"Why, yes, I do believe so," Mr. Willis says. "I believe it's gonna go all the way down past the Porters' place."

"Is that why them odd trucks are out there?"

"Yes, those are the electric company's trucks."

"And is that why nearly everybody in the world's out there actin' all excited right now?"

"You bet they're excited! You should be too, Missy. Run along now, I got work to do." And he shoos me away with the flick of a wrinkled, knobby hand, but he don't gotta tell me twice. If I didn't have the wagon here, I'd run all the way home.

We're gettin' electricity!

I climb up into the wagon and wish I could tell Josy the news. Or Daddy. 'Course they both probably woulda already known. Heck, they'd probably be helpin' the electric company string up the wires.

3

Friendly Snakes

After leaving Main Street, I take the turn onto Jimmy Mack's road, and it don't matter that I've known him all my life, my heart still flutters when his house comes into view.

He comes out onto the porch when I pull up, and we're both all smiles.

"Hey, beautiful," he says, like always, as he steps toward the wagon and reaches to help me down. "I didn't know you were comin' by."

His hand is warm in mine, and he smells of leather and gun powder, and I cain't imagine how I woulda managed if I hadn't come to see him. "Well, I was at the post office, so I figured I'd stop by on my way home," and *why does my voice sound all high-pitched and squealy in front of Jimmy Mack?*

He bows and kisses my hand like we're some kinda royalty, and he says in his best British accent, "Charmed, I'm sure," and I giggle like a schoolgirl playin' shy. Then he grips my hand and pulls, sayin', "Come here. I got somethin' to show ya," and we run around to the back of the house.

We come to a stop near a big boulder by a pond, and

Jimmy crouches down, pullin' me down with him, and he puts his finger over his lips. Then he slowly pushes aside some tall reeds and whispers, "Look, just up ahead there."

It takes me a minute to see it, but when I do, I yelp and jump back, almost fallin' on my behind, and I scramble backward, and I'm screamin' and Jimmy's laughin', and I shout, "What'd you show me that for?! You know I hate snakes!"

Jimmy reaches for me and says, between his laughs, "Aw, June, no, no, no, this one's a good snake. Not venomous or nothin'."

When my heart stops poundin' so much, I let him pull me into a hug, but I'm still fuming. "Scared me half to death, Jimmy."

"I'm sorry, beautiful," he says, smoothin' my hair. "That snake is – *was* – a northern water snake, but I think you scared him off. He's probably swimmin' around in the pond now."

We sit down on the boulder, and Jimmy's eyes are searching the pond for the snake. "Northern water snakes are harmless to people. Matter fact, most snakes we come across here are harmless. Most of 'em eat fish and frogs and rodents and pests." When he spots it, he sits up tall and points. "Look, there he is!"

I watch it slither swiftly through the water, and I try not to shiver, but I still have a healthy fear of snakes. "How do you know he ain't poisonous?" I ask.

"The easiest way to tell is to look at his face," Jimmy says. "First off, the nonvenomous ones have these vertical lines down their mouths, called labial bars, and second, their eyes look friendly."

I laugh at that. "How can a snake's eyes look friendly?"

"They just do. It's hard to explain, but you can see the difference between a venomous snake's eyes and a harmless snake's eyes."

"*If* you wanna get close enough to see the snake's eyes!"

"That's true," Jimmy agrees. "Until you know more about snakes, you probably wanna steer clear of 'em all."

I'm thinkin' that will be no problem for me, no sir, and then Jimmy says, "Naw, but most snakes are good. The only venomous ones you gotta worry about out here are the timber rattler and the copperhead. But even they ain't gonna bite you unless you give 'em a good reason to."

I relax a little, and we watch the snake swim around the edges of the pond and slip stealthily in and out of pondweeds and under sticks and leaves. Grasshoppers buzz and pop around us, and cardinals chirp greetings to each other. I'm thinkin' about how peaceful it is out here when I'm startled by somethin' I see outa the corner of my eye. It's a huge brown bat — probably a fruit bat, but with my luck, I wouldn't be surprised if it was a vampire bat come to attack and kill. It's just hangin' there in a tree, and it scares me more than the "friendly-eyed" snake.

"What's wrong?" Jimmy asks, and all I can do is point.

He looks where I'm pointing. "What? I don't see nothin'."

"It's a giant bat! How can you not see that?"

He gets up and steps slowly toward the tree, peering squinty-eyed at the bat. He's got to see it by now, but he keeps edging toward it, his head pointed forward like a coon hound on the hunt.

"Be careful, Jimmy!"

Then, when he's right up close to it, he snatches it out of the tree just like that and holds it up for me to see.

I jump up in astonishment, thinkin' he has got to be plumb crazy, 'til he shakes it and shouts, "It's a leaf!" Then he bursts out laughin' and I cover my face with my hands, all kinds

13

of embarrassed.

He brings the bat leaf to me and hugs the embarrassment away. In my defense, there's no Godly reason a big brown leaf like that should be hangin' in a green-leafed tree, so of course it looked like a bat.

When Jimmy's finally done laughin', I remember why I came over here in the first place. "Say, Jimmy, did you hear we're gettin' electricity in Maynardville and out to the farms? Mr. Willis at the post office said the president signed some law that will help rural towns and farms get electricity."

Jimmy shakes his head. "The president ain't got nothin' to do with it. It's the townsfolk that are makin' it happen."

"What do you mean?"

"A bunch of 'em are gettin' together to form an electric co-op. Mr. Tomlinson – you know he's runnin' for mayor – anyway, he's heading it up, so you should talk to him. The plan is to get everyone in Maynardville and out past your farm to sign on."

I think about what Margaret Ann has told me about her new life in Nashville, which includes having electricity in the house, and I start to get excited about it. She said she can pull a chain from the ceiling and a light comes on. And they can cook without puttin' wood into a woodstove. And they can plug in an iron and it gets hot just like that.

"Well, where do I sign up?" It sounds magical to me.

"Talk to Mr. Tomlinson. I'll go with you. You just have to be able to pay the electric bill."

My heart sinks. Pay the bill? We're havin' a hard enough time payin' the mortgage and buyin' gas for the car. We cain't afford anything else.

"I guess I'll have to talk to Mama first," I say, and then I realize I'd better get on home and get to my chores before

Mama gets home from work. This is her half-day.

We walk back toward Jimmy's house, and a gust of cool wind blows my hair in my face. We both look up, and the sky is an eerie green-gray with mean-lookin' clouds.

"Best get home before that opens up," Jimmy says. "Wait, I almost forgot. I got somethin' for ya," and he hops up the porch steps two at a time.

"It ain't another snake is it?" I holler out, but he's already stompin' into the house. When he bounds back out, he's got a book in his hand.

"My ma got this for me, and I figured you'd like it. It's brand-new. Just published."

I take it and read the cover. "*Mary Poppins*. Did you read it?"

"You know I ain't much of a reader," Jimmy says, "but you are, so it's yours."

I smile, run my hand over the book cover, feel its spine, lift it up and smell the paper, which I know Jimmy thinks is weird, but I cain't help it. Then I step up on my tiptoes and kiss Jimmy on the cheek.

"Thank you, Jimmy. You're so thoughtful." It reminds me of the day I came over here with Margaret Ann, with my newly cut hair and my boy's disguise, and we told Jimmy about my mission to hop a train, and he gave me that leather pack to carry my belongings in. It was so kind of him. He's always been that way. Generous. Thoughtful. Even when we were little.

I remember one time, I couldn'ta been more than seven years old or thereabouts, so Jimmy woulda been about ten or eleven – he was almost the same age as Josy. We were at the farmers' market, and I had my arms full of jars of jam. I cain't remember why I was carryin' jars of jam like that, but there I was, totin' at least six of 'em from one wagon to another, and

I tripped and all the jars tumbled to the ground. It was grass, so nothin' broke, but I was so angry at myself that I started cryin', and Jimmy Mack appeared outa nowhere – and even back then, I thought he was the bees knees – and he gathered up the jars and carried them for me like a hero (at least, that's how it felt to my seven-year-old self). And then to make me feel better, he pulled out a caramel cube from his pocket and gave it to me, and I do believe that was the day that caramel cubes became my favorite candy in the world.

As I settle myself in the wagon and grab the reins, Jimmy hollers, "June. Watch out for all them bats on the way home." And he grins like he got away with somethin', and I wave and head home, with one eye on the sky for storm clouds and one eye on the ground for snakes. And if I'm tellin' the truth, I'm also lookin' closely at the leaves on the trees. But mostly, I'm thinkin' that Jimmy has friendly eyes just like the snake's, and I love that he gave me a book for no reason. I cain't wait to get home and finish my chores so I can read *Mary Poppins*.

4

It Don't Make No Sense

The wind is blowin' somethin' awful by the time I pull up the drive. I take Molly straight to the barn and unhitch the wagon. My hair's whippin' around my face as I guide her into her stall, and one of the barn doors swings shut with a clatter, makin' poor Molly whinny and buck.

"It's okay, ol' girl," I coo, petting her softly. "But you better get in here and let me go into the house, 'cause it's about to storm like nobody's business." I make sure she's got water and straw, and then I close and secure the barn doors as they fight against me in the wind.

The green-gray sky is darker now, the wind louder, and rain starts comin' down hard – so hard it hurts. But it don't take me a second of lookin' down at the ground to see that it ain't just rain – it's hail, too.

Mary Poppins tucked inside my pants waist, I run to the chicken coop, where the chickens are squawkin' up a fuss, but at least they're smart enough to stay inside. I grab the feeders that were outside and secure them in the coop, then go around and shut the windows and the door, and I'm gettin' pummeled by hail the whole time, screamin' and tryin' to cover my head with my arms. And just as fast as it started, the hail stops. But the rain is still comin' down in furious sheets.

I'm pantin' and lookin' up at the angry clouds when Mama comes rumbling up in the Model T, and she jumps down practically before it even rolls to a stop.

"You alright, June?" she hollers as she grabs some bags from the car and starts jogging toward the house. Somethin' in the wind makes her stop. Makes us both stop and look up.

"Mama, what's that?" Over the trees that line the drive is a whirl of dust so big it scares me somethin' awful.

Mama drops her bags. "Get to the cellar! Now!" she hollers, and we run, her tugging me along as I watch the swirling sky behind us. She pulls open the cellar door, and that's when I hear the pathetic, whimpering mewl of a cat.

"Bug!" She's scampering toward the barn, and I take one glance at Mama and see her "Don't you dare" look before I take off after the cat. Mama hollers my name until the sound of her voice is swallowed by the whipping wind as the tornado topples trees on its way toward us.

Bug is hunkered down by the barn doors, and she screeches as I scoop her up and run back toward the cellar. I don't look behind me, but I can feel debris flyin' around me, and I know the tornado is so close, and then somethin' hits the back of my leg and I trip and fall.

"June!" Mama yells, but in the roar of the wind, she sounds like a whisper.

I lose hold of Bug when I stumble to the hail-covered ground, and I holler 'cause I cain't even see her no more. The wind feels like it's 'bout to pick me right off the ground, and I claw at the ground and crawl the rest of the way.

When I reach the cellar, Mama grabs my arm and pulls me

down the steps, and I don't even have to pull the door closed 'cause the wind throws it shut, and just when I'm about to cry 'cause I lost Bug, I hear her mewl.

"Bug!"

"She ran right in after you fell," Mama says, and me and Mama huddle together in the dark, pantin' from exhaustion and shakin' in fear. I know I musta been a second away from gettin' tossed around by that tornado, and I thank God I made it, and I silently thank Mama for not scoldin' me for going back for Bug.

The wind howls. The ground beneath our feet creaks and shakes. There's clanging and bumping louder than anything I ever heard. We crouch down when it sounds like the ground above our head is gonna cave in on us, and Mama starts prayin' out loud. She prays for what seems like hours, but I know it must only be minutes, and suddenly it's quiet, save for Bug's mewlin'. We straighten up, an inch at a time, as if we're afraid the tornado's gonna come back.

Mama lets go of me and moves toward the steps.

"Wait! Mama," my throat catches. "What if— what if—"

"Oh, June," she says, and I can hear tears in her voice. "Come take my hand. We'll go together."

I reach toward her voice, find her hand, and grab it with all my life. I'm so scared to walk up those steps and see what's left – or not left – of our home.

When Mama pushes the door open, blinding light falls into the cellar, and I almost laugh. How can a tornado rip through with its destruction one minute and the sun shine its brightness the next? It don't make no sense.

We emerge from underground, and my eyes go first to the house. It's still standing, thank God. Then I look toward the mule barn. Still there. We exhale sharply, and I grab Mama in a hug.

"It's okay! We're okay!"

"Praise the Lord," Mama says.

And we smile into the sun. Somethin' pinches my waist, and I'm surprised to find *Mary Poppins* still tucked in there, a little wet and beat up, but whole at least.

Then we get a closer look around at what's not whole.

5

What's Not Whole

We move in slow motion, turning this way and that, scanning the land, noticing things out of place, things missing. Where there should be the clucking of chickens, the twitter of birds, the buzzing of late summer bugs, the only sound is the dying wind.

The chicken coop is gone. "Where are the chickens?" I ask Mama. There's not a scrap of wood, a crumb of chicken feed, a single feather. It's like it never existed.

Mama makes a sound like a cry of pain, and I follow her eyes. A tree limb sticks out of the roof of the house, like a dagger right through the heart.

Down the drive, branches are scattered like a game of pick-up sticks, one poking right through the windows of the car, the rest of the tree crushing the car with its weight. Wire fencing is twisted around tree trunks and balled up on the ground like so much metal tumbleweed.

Shingles and shrubs, fence posts and firewood, metal odds and ends, dirt churned up in piles – it all covers the ground in such randomness, it reminds me of one of those games where you have to search and find a list of items in a picture. And dirty! Everything's so dirty, as if the whole farm done took a mud bath.

Then it hits me that I don't hear a noise from the mule barn. I race to the barn, my mind a mess of fear and hope all at the same time, and I cain't breathe until I unlatch the doors and see Molly's big ol' ears twitching above the wall of her stall.

"Thank God!" I let out a woosh of air and turn the corner to see Molly just chompin' on straw like ain't nothin' wrong, just a regular ol' day. I grab her head in my hands and put my forehead on her nose. "Molly, you sweet, silly girl!" She huffs and wraps her head over my shoulder, and I swear if ever anybody's feeling scared or stressed, a hug from a mule is the best medicine.

"June." Mama's there suddenly, her hand on my back. "Let's go make sure everything's okay with the house, and then I think we should go to town. See if anybody needs anything."

We look at each other, the implications looming ominously overhead. My thoughts go to Jimmy, then to Maynardville and the church and the school, and all our friends, and I snap into action. "You're right. Let's go."

I open the stall and nudge Molly out, wondering if the wagon is still in one piece on the side of the barn. I cross my fingers and then scold myself for actin' like a little kid, but I'm relieved when I turn the corner and see the wagon's alright. Me and Mama get Molly hitched up and then walk her over to the house.

We stand facing the porch for a moment, afraid to go in.

"Maybe we should walk around to the back first," Mama says. "Check the walls and structure on the outside. If it looks alright, then we go in."

"Sounds good to me." We link arms, and just as we're heading around the side, Bug trots up and joins us, lookin' lost and confused. I shake my head. "Sorry, Bug, but I ain't pickin' you up right now, 'cause you look like you just rolled around in a pit of mud."

"I think we're all gonna look like that over the next few days, June." She says it like she wants to laugh about it, but her face is serious.

We don't find any huge problems with the house, other than the tree branch stabbin' the roof – just some busted windows and a whole lot of mud. A few of our things nearest the busted windows are knocked over, and there's glass on the floor, but everything else looks just like we left it.

I run to my bedroom and go straight to the wardrobe, fish around behind my hangin' clothes 'til I feel a small wooden box. I bring it out gently, like it's the most fragile thing in the world. In a way it is. This box is where I've kept Josy's purple marble since Paul returned it to me. I figured it'd be better if I kept it in a safe place. That day, I found a tiny wooden box layin' out on the ground by the old general store, and I picked it up, deciding it would be a perfect hiding place for my marble.

I rub my thumb across the smooth wood. The hinge creaks when I open it, and I let out a relieved breath to see the beautiful marble sittin' there where it should be. Silly, I know. Ain't no reason why it would be gone when the wardrobe isn't even near a window and is perfectly intact. But still, I had to check.

Mama peeks her head around my door. "Let's go on to town now."

I'm not prepared for what I see as we creep along in the wagon, steering Molly around fallen trees and debris. The poles that lined the road, ready to string up the electric wires someday soon – well they're all over the place now. I can see one way out in the field, and one's clear on the other side of the road, and others are just gone, I guess.

We can see ruts in the ground that dot the path the tornado took, sweeping everything out of its way: wooden planks, metal rods, roof shingles, fencing, bricks, what looks like car parts, a twisted-up bicycle.

"Lord almighty, I hope no one was hurt," Mama says. My thoughts turn back to Jimmy, and I find myself crossing my fingers again.

And that's when we see a cow and a pig come trottin' along down the road, and I cain't help it, I let a laugh escape. Despite the seriousness of what has happened, despite the gravity of what we may still find, the sight of those silly animals prancin' along like they're up to something is just about the funniest thing I ever did see. Mama smiles for a split second but then wipes it away.

"Those belong to the Porters," she says. "We'll go by there later and let 'em know."

I watch as they pass us up, glancin' at us and almost noddin' to say hello. "Shoot, Mama, they may just walk on home on their own."

Then I wonder how they got all the way out here, and I don't want to think about that, 'cause if a single tornado can blow eighteen hundred pounds of animal that far from home, what could it have done to the people who live in town?

6

Heart and Soul

When we pass the road that leads to Margaret Ann's house, I have the urge to go check on her, even though I know she don't live there no more. No one lives there, and Mama says the bank owns that house. I peer down the road anyway, wonderin' if the bank's house is still standing, and it looks like it is.

Pastor Klein's car is in front of the church, and he's standin' on the steps with his hands on his hips. Mama stops the wagon and we clamber down. "Be careful," Mama says as we step over and around piles of I-don't-know-what-all.

"I'll tell ya, Mrs. Baker," Pastor Klein says, "the Lord sure was lookin' out for Maynardville."

"Is that right?" Mama asks, relief in her voice.

Pastor Klein waves a hand toward the church, inviting us to look around, and I cain't even believe it. The whole town is drenched in mud, but the white clapboard church house is pristine. Looks like it's been washed clean.

"Not a lick of damage to the church or the school," he says, wonder in his voice.

"Well, ain't that a blessing!" Mama says, her face spreading into a smile.

"That school house was built in eighteen-fifty-five, mind you, by a man named Lester McBride. That was before our city's name was changed from Liberty to Maynardville. McBride built the school house in honor of his wife's family – the Glasses – who settled in the area with seven children but couldn't make the long walk to the nearest school."

Seeing my eyes light up, Pastor Klein adds, "You guessed it. Our very own Miss Glass – your teacher – is one of the grandchildren of Mr. Bixby Glass, Lester McBride's father-in-law." He shakes his head. "Anyhow, ain't nothin' gonna blow that little school away. McBride built it out of local lumber, heart, and soul."

"When was the church built, Pastor Klein?" I ask, noticing there ain't a single scratch on the windows or the door.

"Nineteen-oh-four," he says, "and it has withstood so many threats." He turns to Mama. "You remember the fire of nineteen-fifteen that burnt up acres and acres but didn't touch the church?"

"I do. I was fourteen or fifteen, I think."

"By the grace of God," Pastor Klein says. "Today, we coulda had a lot of deaths, homes destroyed, people hurt. But, ladies, we have been surely blessed."

"You mean everybody's okay?" I ask, and at the same time, Mama asks, "There's no damage?"

Pastor Klein smiles and says, "Far as I know, nobody in Maynardville is hurt, and all our homes are still standin'. 'Course, there's a little damage here and there. You folks saw the scattered mess on your way over, I suppose."

We nod, and now we're able to smile and laugh 'cause it sounds like our farm got the worst of it, and we are so relieved that everybody in Maynardville is alright.

"It may take 'em longer to get the electricity strung up now, but we've waited this long – I don't suppose an extra week or two or four's gonna matter much."

"You're right, Pastor Klein," Mama says, and she squeezes his arm and thanks him and tells him we're goin' to check on friends, and we climb back into the wagon and head to Main Street, not quite knowin' what to say. On the one hand, we want to be thankful, but on the other hand, we want to see for ourselves, make sure what the pastor said is true.

Other folks musta had the same idea, 'cause downtown is full of people walkin' around, peekin' in shop windows, pullin' tree limbs outa the road, sweepin' the sidewalk. While Mama talks to folks, I hear the same exclamations everywhere. *Thank God no one was hurt! It's a miracle there wasn't more damage. It's incredible how that tornado zipped around and left everything still standing.*

I wonder if any of them lost their whole chicken coop, chickens and all, or have a big tree limb stickin' straight up outa the roof of their house or have broken windows and glass shattered everywhere. But I don't say nothin'.

The tornado's all anyone talks about for days afterward. The roadside is packed with the hustle and bustle of folks clearing away debris, cuttin' up limbs and broken trees, and combing the grounds like they're searching for treasure.

Mr. and Mrs. Porter's rogue cow and pig made it home alright. Turns out the tornado didn't blow 'em away. They got out hours before, and the storm got 'em all scared and disoriented.

Me and Mama spend a few days helpin' neighbors clean up messes the storm left behind, and those neighbors help us replace the broken windows and patch the roof. Mama cain't go to work on accounta the car bein' damaged, so now we're back to the days when we were scramblin' to make ends meet, and that makes my heart hurt.

"We were headin' down this road anyhow, June, what with gas and maintenance on the car and all," Mama says, "but we'll make it. We always do."

7

Jimmy Mack Ain't Jimmy Mack

It's been five days since the tornado, and the weather has been as pleasant as can be. Today's one of those cloudless, clear-blue days that you can see the big, white moon against the sky even though it's the middle of the afternoon.

My heart is as full as that crazy moon as I watch Jimmy hammer the last nail into the chicken coop we're building together. We ain't got chickens for it yet, but this coop is the best thing I've laid eyes on in I-don't-know-how-long.

"What color you wanna paint it?" Jimmy asks.

"I guess that depends on what colors ya got." I cross my fingers that he has purple, even though that's downright silly. Who ever seen a purple chicken coop?

"We've got red, white, and a little bit of yella – but this coop's not that big. Should be plenty."

"Can we make it yellow *and* white?" I'm grinning from ear

to ear, and somehow I know that Jimmy would paint this thing in his own blood if I asked him to. He's just that kind. Jimmy has become more than just some ol' boyfriend. He's become my best friend since Margaret Ann moved away, and that's sayin' somethin' 'cause I don't make friends too easily.

There are some other girls around my age who live nearby, but I don't connect with them the way I connected with Margaret Ann. One of 'em, Nancy Brown, is the kind of person who'll pinch you ninety-seven times on St. Patrick's Day, even after you tell her to stop. Another one, Bertha Bellows, is always sayin' bad things about people, and one time when I heard her bad-mouthin' Miss Glass, that was the end of even thinkin' about bein' her friend. And then there's Barbara, who likes to take my biscuits at lunch when I have extra, 'cause she says my biscuits are the best she's ever tasted. I don't mind sharin', but she don't ever share any of her food with me, like Margaret Ann always did.

So Jimmy fills the void that Margaret Ann left, and I'm perfectly fine with that, 'cause the bonus is that he's the cutest boy in Union County, and all them other girls are 'bout swallowed up with jealousy. Now, I ain't the gloatin' type, but I sure do smile inside when we're at school and Jimmy holds my hand and one of them shoots green monster eyes my way.

We stand and admire the chicken coop, and Jimmy says, "Let's eat first, paint second." So we head for the front porch, where we left a picnic basket. While he sets out the sausage and rolls, I go to the cellar and get us some semi-cool lemonade.

As we settle ourselves with our plates in our laps, a purple martin lands on the porch railing, and it twitches and ducks its head side to side like it's checkin' out what we got to offer. It reminds me of the time me and Jimmy were walkin' down the lane, and a male purple martin was chasin' a female one around in the air, flyin' low, and then suddenly the male knocked the female to the ground, and then, I ain't even exaggeratin', that male puffed out his chest and held out his wings and started prancin' around like *Look at me! Look at what I can do!* If the female had eyes like ours, she woulda rolled 'em, I bet, 'cause I swear it looked like she wasn't gonna give the poor fella the time of day. She just took off without a backward glance, and that sad, rejected martin sat there lookin' around for a moment before flyin' away.

At the time, Jimmy had said, "See? Males of all species gotta show off to the ladies."

"Yeah? Lemme see you do a dance for me, then." I'd been teasin', but right then and there, in the middle of the lane, Jimmy did a little jig that I will never forget.

"I don't deserve you," I say all of a sudden, as we sit there watchin' that purple martin on the porch railing and it flies away.

"What?" Jimmy looks at me like I got two heads.

I blush and look down at the food in my lap. "I don't know why I said that, I just …"

He's still lookin' at me, and for some reason I feel like cryin'. Finally I look at him, but I cain't hold eye contact, so I look at the chicken coop. "You have done so much for me. Been so kind and generous. I don't feel like I deserve that."

"When did you first know we belong together?" Jimmy asks.

I'm shocked by the complete change of subject. And I don't know how to answer, because I've been dotin' on Jimmy Mack since as far back as I can remember, but I don't think I want him to know that. Do I? I think back to the time Margaret Ann cut my hair and we went to test my get-up on Jimmy, and he gave me that leather pack. I know I felt something then, but he was with Margaret Ann at the time, so it would be wildly inappropriate for me to voice what I felt. So I think of another answer.

"Well, back when Margaret Ann moved away ... we had already grown so close as friends," I say, putting my hand up to block the sun from my eyes, but really more to hide my eyes from Jimmy. "And you were so kind to me."

He looks at me like he's waitin' for more. "And?"

I'm gigglin' outa embarrassment now, but I go ahead and say, "As much as I love Margaret Ann and didn't want her to leave, I—"

"You what?" He's smilin' now, and I'm so embarrassed that I look away, up, down, everywhere but at Jimmy.

"I guess I felt like she was meant to go... for us." He's starin' so intently at me now, and I'm blushin' like mad. "Stop it, Jimmy!"

When the gigglin' winds down, he says, "You know when I first knew we belong together?"

"When?" I'm almost afraid to hear his answer.

"The first time I ever saw you. At the farmer's market."

"What? But we were just kids then."

"I know. But I still knew."

"Well, how come you never said nothin', then?"

He sighs a long sigh and lifts his shoulders like he's gonna do the usual boy thing and just shrug. So I'm shocked when he says, "You have always been something of a mystery to me. You're tough and strong, but also feminine and gentle. You're a rebel, but also a good, kindhearted person. You miss so much school, but you're smarter than anyone I know. You're soft and quiet, but you'll rip the head off of anyone that does you wrong."

I gaze at him, unsure of where he's going with this.

"To be all those things at once, well, I guess that's always been sort of intimidating to me."

I think on that a spell, watch as a little yellow butterfly lands on my knee. I softly scoop my hand underneath it, and it flutters up onto my knuckles. Finally, I say, "Maybe I don't need a label. I'm label-less. Undefinable."

As I watch the butterfly flit away, Jimmy leans close and kisses me on my cheekbone. "The only definition I can think of for you is *perfect*."

Now with my stomach doin' flips, I look down and notice that we haven't eaten a bite of our lunch. Then I turn to see Mama easing the screen door open, and I wonder how much she heard. Not that it matters, really. We're so close and all. But this conversation has me so flummoxed, and I think knowin' Mama heard the whole thing would be even more embarrassing. Mama's raised eyebrows tell me she notices that my face is beet red and she musta heard at least some of it.

"Y'all 'bout done with the chicken coop?" she asks.

"Yes, Mrs. Baker," Jimmy says, in his proper way he always talks to Mama, even though he's known her all his life. "We just stopped for lunch, and then all we gotta do is paint it."

"And add some chickens," I add.

"Well, that's where we're in luck," Mama says. "I heard from Mrs. Porter, and she has family out yonder that have a whole mess of chicks that they're bringin' up. She said we can have four hens and a rooster if we make her some clothes and blankets."

"That's great, Mama!" Four chickens! *And* a rooster. That'll really help us out. But then I remember that Mama don't work at the clothes factory no more, so we don't have the sewin' machine. Or money to buy what we'd need to make clothes and blankets.

As usual, Mama knows just what I'm thinkin', and she says, "Mrs. Tomlinson has a machine that she's willin' to give me since she's gettin' on in age. I'm gonna take the wagon up to get it in a bit. Finish up your lunch and you can come with me." She trots down the steps and heads to the mule barn.

I'm so excited, I start crammin' food into my mouth. Jimmy laughs and says, "I'll have the chicken coop painted by the time you get back."

I throw my arms around him. "Thank you, Jimmy Mack!"

He takes my arms and pulls back so we're lookin' at each other. "You know my name's not Jimmy Mack, right?"

"What?!" What in the world is he talkin' about?

"Well, my name is Jimmy, short for James, but my last name is Mackenroe. Years ago, the guys started callin' me Jimmy Mack, short for Jimmy Mackenroe."

I'm floored. I always thought his name was Jimmy Mack Prescott, or some kind of movie-star name like that.

"That's—I don't even know what to say!" *How did I not know this? What a terrible girlfriend I am.*

"It's no big deal. I just wanted to make sure you knew," he says. "You know, since we belong together and all."

I pinch his shoulder playfully, then swallow down the rest of my lunch and bound off toward Mama and Molly. *Jimmy Mack ain't even Jimmy Mack. How about that?* And that's all I'm thinkin' about now. Plus the last name Mackenroe, and how nice it sounds. After June.

8

JimBoJoe

Dearest June,
Of course I think Paul should pay for what
he did to Josy, but I don't see how. He's railroad police,
and Josy was breaking the law, and now it will be your
word against the police's. All I know is you need to be
real careful. In other news, there's drama here at Tilly's
— that's the beauty parlor. The owner had to let someone
go, and the lady he let go was awfully sore about it
because she thought it should have been me. Now it's
spread all around town that she wants to get even with
me. Me! I'm only 16! Anyway, there's also trouble in
Paradise. Say-Lynn's boyfriend dumped her already.
Said she was too much to take. Imagine that. A
Murphy, too much to take. Well, I gotta go now. Ain't
you got a telephone yet? Wish I could call and talk to
you on your birthday.
Friends forever,
M. A.

I got her letter on the first of July, and it's been three days and I ain't stopped thinkin' about it since. Matter fact, as I sit here with Jimmy at the Fourth of July picnic in Maynardville, I must look grumpy, 'cause he keeps askin' me what's wrong. I don't tell him what Margaret Ann said about Josy breakin' the law. I just tell him I'm thinkin' about Josy.

There's not much shade in the farmer's market field where we have our picnic every year, so me and Jimmy are sittin' under the tent where Mrs. Linder set up her desserts. We're battin' away bees and flies while little kids jump around with cupcake frosting on their mouths, and littler kids are throwin' fits 'cause their mama won't let them have a second helping. Out in the field, a group of men are playin' horseshoes, some kids are spittin' watermelon seeds, girls are gigglin' behind cupped hands, mamas are chasin' their babies around, and grammas and grampas are fannin' themselves against the heat.

I used to cherish these days. I cain't remember a time the Fourth of July picnic wasn't my favorite event. But now, I don't know. All I see are bees and flies and sweat, and I don't like it.

"It's hard to enjoy it without your brother here, huh?" Jimmy says.

I think on that awhile, and then I realize how selfish I've been. Josy was Jimmy's friend once upon a time. He must miss him too, and I ain't even asked him how he feels.

"You used to hang out with Josy," I say, not sure how to broach the subject. "Are you—I mean, do you miss him?"

"You might not remember, but me, your brother, and a boy named Bo were best friends a long time ago." Jimmy smiles, as if remembering good ol' days. "The three of us went everywhere together. To the lake, the woods, runnin' around town like the Three Musketeers or somethin'. People 'round town got so used to seein' us three together, they called us JimBoJoe, like all one name. 'Oh, look out, here come JimBoJoe!'"

"Did y'all ever break the law?"

Jimmy looks surprised, but chuckles and says, "Nah, we were good kids. But Bo would sweet-talk his way to some free candy for the three of us. We loved playin' tricks on folks, like settin' off firecrackers in a bucket so they sounded like gunshots. And sometimes when some guys were playin' ball in the field out behind the gas station, we'd nick one of their extra balls they had layin' there."

"What?! That's awful!" I'm appalled, but Jimmy's just laughin' it up.

"We'd hightail it outa there faster than you ever seen anyone run. And then we'd have a ball to play with."

"I never saw you come around the farm much. And Josy never told me about all your shenanigans."

"Well, like I said, it was a long time ago. Bo and his family moved away, and your brother got so busy with farm stuff, and we just..." He trails off and looks kinda sad. "No more JimBoJoe," he finally says, and that's when I see it ain't sadness, it's regret in his eyes.

I'm about to tell him I'm sorry, when two little girls come over beggin' me to play hide-and-seek with them.

"Please, June, Pleeeease?" they beg when I start to resist.

"Go on, June," Jimmy says. "You can't let these sweet kids down, can you?"

"Oh, okay, but just one round." But my words are swallowed up by their cheerin' and clappin'. I try to be cheerful as we play, but now I cain't shake the thought of Josy doin' dishonest things when he was younger. I wonder if he did anything dishonest when he was out on the rails. Could that have led to— no, I don't want to think about that.

But the "JimBoJoe" story sticks with me. I imagine the three of them runnin' around and causin' trouble and havin' fun, and I love these images I've created in my head so much, that when Mama brings home the hens and rooster we were promised, I name that rooster JimBoJoe.

9

The Sweetest Sixteen

When we hit September, I start thinkin' about my birthday. Sixteen. For most girls, that's a big deal. When Margaret Ann turned sixteen, her family went all out, she told me in one of her letters. There was cake and ice cream, lots of gifts, and their whole house was decorated in streamers and balloons and paper flowers. Most girls dress up real pretty – maybe even get a new dress for their "Sweet Sixteen."

But I ain't like most girls. Most girls didn't lose their brother and daddy one after the other, and most girls aren't hangin' on by a thread with their depressed mama in their depressed house in a depressed town in the middle of a financial depression. Or maybe they are, I don't know. Maybe I'm silly and selfish to think I'm the only one going through something terribly awful on my sixteenth birthday. Whatever the case, the closer it gets to my birthday, the more anxious I get, 'cause I know it's a big-deal birthday, but I don't feel like having a big-deal celebration.

I miss Josy and Daddy somethin' awful, and thinkin' about

what they woulda done for my Sweet Sixteen brings fat tears to my eyes and a painful lump in my throat and stomach. Daddy woulda taken me to Knoxville for an ice cream, and Josy woulda brought me a whole handful of caramel cubes. We'd probably put on the radio and dance on the porch in the September breeze. There'd be no fancy dress, but there'd be a house overflowing with love and happiness.

Mama seems to sense what I'm feelin', so she skirts around the topic. I think she's only brought it up one time this month, when she asked me if I wanted anything special. At the time, I couldn't think of anything special I wanted, other than to be able to talk to Margaret Ann on a telephone, but that's impossible – or so I thought.

Three exciting things happen during my birthday month, despite my feelin' so sad. The first exciting thing happens about the middle of September. Electricity is strung to the house! You wouldn't think that one little ol' lightbulb would be a life-changing thing, but let me tell you, me and Mama cain't get over the novelty of pullin' a chain in the kitchen and lightin' up the whole front of the house. They even put one in our bedrooms and the washroom. Now we only have to use the lanterns if we go outside after dark.

The first few days after the lights were put in, we just about wore out those chains. I would pull it for sheer fascination, and then Mama would pull it to "save electricity," but sure enough, she'd pull it again a few minutes later and smile real big and say, "Who would have ever thought we'd have such luxuries out here on our farm?"

But the honest-to-God biggest luxury of all, even more than bein' able to light up the house, is bein' able to cool it up. A few days before my birthday, when it's way too hot to be September, Mama brings home an electric fan, and that's the second exciting thing. We plug it into the outlet the electric company installed in the front room, and I ain't even exaggeratin' when I say we are in pure Heaven sittin' on the sofa with that fan blowin' in our faces. We sure will make use of that fan next summertime, if we don't wear it plumb out before then.

On the morning of my birthday, I'm feelin' like we already got everything we need ('cept Josy and Daddy, of course), but when I shuffle into the kitchen, wiping the sleep outa my eyes, Mama's sittin' at the table with a big smile on her face, and there in front of her is a contraption we ain't never had in our house before. It's a telephone! This is the third exciting thing. Mama jumps up and wraps her arms around my shoulders.

"Happy birthday, June."

"Is that a telephone? How's it work?"

Mama picks it up and puts it on a counter in the kitchen and connects it to the wall. "Well, when they brought the electric wires out here, they also brought a telephone line." She grins and lets out a breath like she done run a mile. "Now, let's see if it works."

She takes a piece of paper out of her apron pocket. "I've got Margaret Ann's telephone number here."

I gasp. "You do? Oh, thank you, Mama!"

"Alright, now, what you have to do is pick up the receiver like this, and you should get the operator, and you tell her you want to reach this number." She holds the paper out to me.

I can barely contain my excitement when I unhook the cup from its holder and bring it to my ear, and after a pop of static, I'm amazed to hear a woman speaking to me. I bring the candlestick part of the telephone closer to me and practically shout into the speaker.

"I need to reach NA-five, one-one-three-seven."

The woman tells me she's connecting me, and there's another pop and crackle, and lo and behold, someone answers on the other end.

"Hello, this is June Baker, and I'm calling for Margaret Ann Murphy."

"June?! Why, this is Margaret Ann! Is this really June?"

I'm laughin' and talkin' at the same time now. "Yes! Yes! Hi, Margaret Ann! It's me!"

"And it's your birthday! Happy sixteenth! You got a telephone?"

"Yes, Mama hooked it up just now so I could call you."

And we share a few moments of breathless exhilaration and fast talkin' before Mama says I need to hang up so's it don't cost too much, and then Margaret Ann wants to know our telephone number so she can call me sometime.

"Mama, what's our telephone number?" I whisper, and then I'm repeatin' what she says into the speaker. We both say "Bye!" about twenty times before finally hanging up, and I have the widest grin stuck on my face.

Jimmy comes over later, and after marveling at the telephone, he pulls a small wrapped box out of his jacket pocket. "For you, June."

I take the box and pull open the ribbons. "Aww, you didn't have to get me nothin'."

When I lift the lid, I see the most perfect little yellow butterfly with purple fringe. As I lift it out of the box's cushion, Jimmy says, "It's a bookmark. See this part here's a magnet, so when you attach it to the page you're on, it won't fall out."

"Oh my gosh, Jimmy, it's wonderful!" I run to my room to get a book, and then I clip the butterfly magnet over a page and admire the cascade of purple fringe that hangs over the cover of the book when I close it. I show it off to Mama, who, of course, loves it too.

I walk Jimmy onto the porch before he leaves, and he holds his arm out in front of me. "Wait! We need to be careful. I see an awful lot of bats out here."

"Jimmy!" I pinch his arm and play mad until he begs for forgiveness. I'm left with his scent of leather and gun powder – and is that cologne I smell? And as he rides away on his bicycle, I grin from ear to ear.

I cain't get over it. On my sixteenth birthday, I've made my first telephone call, we have electricity in our house for the first time, and my first real boyfriend has given me the most thoughtful gift. It's been the sweetest Sweet Sixteen ever.

10

I've Handled Worse

Now that the wind has turned cold and the leaves have fallen, it seems like everyone done plumb forgot about the tornado. Thanksgiving's come and gone, and now everyone's in the Christmas spirit. They hang tinsel over busted awnings and wreaths over stripped paint. And leaves cover up rivets in the ground, so what evidence there was of any damage is disguised as holiday cheer.

There's a spindly little ol' tree by the corner of the road that goes to Jimmy's house that looks like it don't belong, 'cause all the trees around it are tall, monstrous things. Every winter, somebody decorates the little tree with Christmas garland and sparkly ornaments. It's funny – this tiny town where everybody knows everybody else's business, and nobody knows who decorates that tree. And it's been happenin' for ages. I cain't remember a time when that tree didn't turn up all sweet and shiny for the holidays. I like to think Josy and Daddy got somethin' to do with it now. I know that's silly, but it helps me.

Even Mama seems to be in the Christmas spirit, but I suspect she's play-acting for my sake. And it works. A week ago, we were both so swallowed up with grief it felt like we had nothing left in the world, and now, just like the snap of a finger, it's like it's me and Mama, two heroes against the world. Sitting on top of the world.

Mama's been making herbal remedies, and I had no idea they'd be so popular. All of Maynardville wants to buy what Mama makes. At first it earned just enough money to turn around and buy the bottles to put the herbs in and tend to the herb garden, but now we got customers on a waitlist and change to spare. So I been helpin' a lot with that when I ain't in school, and I even got Jimmy runnin' errands for us. He helped us close in the back porch and make the herb garden so's it'll still grow in the winter's cold.

All this work and excitement darn near swallowed up any time to grieve over another Christmas without Josy and Daddy, and I don't mind sayin' that I'm grateful for that. To be honest, I'm tired of being sad and cryin' and wishin' we could go back to normal, back to the days before Josy left to ride the rails. I discovered that it's more exhaustin' to be sad than it is to be happy. So maybe I'll just take the easy way out from now on and be happy without frettin' over anything. That sounds like the best plan, and it makes me smile inside to finally decide that I'm over all the loss we suffered and ready to live my life and be happy.

> *Dearest June,*
> *I am happy to hear that you are doing so well. It's just the greatest thing ever to finally hear that you're smiling again and living again. I was so worried about you with all that you've been through. Maybe you can*

come visit me soon.

Not much is going on here – just the same old same old. Except we had this terrible dust storm a few months ago. I never seen anything like it. They say it started down in Texas and blew all the way over here. Did you see it from your house? We had to stay inside all day, and everything was covered in red dust afterward – the windows and everything! Sometimes the sky looks dirty and rusty, and Mama says it's because of the drought down yonder, and there've been folks passing through here looking for good farmland. It's just terrible.

Well, I'll bet you got better things to do than read about dust, so I'll let you go and hope we get to see each other soon. Hope you had a happy Thanksgiving! Tell your mama and Jimmy I said hello.

Friends forever,
M.A.

"What's next for us, Mama?"

We're sittin' on the back porch one Sunday afternoon, admiring the rows and rows of tiny bottles of herbs and teas and tonics we made, probably enough to pay this month's mortgage and taxes combined. The early December wind is icy, but the bright sun warms the goose bumps right off.

"What do you mean, what's next?" Mama asks with a frown.

Her question throws me. I mean, once you've made a success at somethin', don't you want to go even further? Doesn't everybody?

46

"Well, look at what we've done with the remedies, and it all started a couple of years ago with your tiny herb garden. Now it's…" I wave my hand with a flourish at everything around us on the enclosed back porch that's more of an herb greenhouse now, and the bottles that we never imagined anybody would pay money for. "Couldn't we open a shop downtown? We could call it … Baker's Apothecary!"

Mama laughs. "Oh, June. Always lookin' for the next big thing, aren't you?"

"Aren't *you*?"

Mama shakes her head. "I think those days are over for me. Maybe you can open a shop someday, but me? Now? I don't know if they'd even let me. A woman ownin' a shop downtown. Imagine that."

This way of thinking angers me. "I don't wanna just imagine it. I want to do it!"

"I know," Mama sighs. "But I'm happy just where we are. I don't need the next big thing, and frankly don't have the energy for it."

I look away, unable to understand her. It's like she's given up on things. I know she hasn't really, but it's crazy to me that she can be content at a standstill.

"June." Mama puts gentle hands on my shoulders and turns me toward her. "You have a fire in you that I truly admire, and I don't ever want you to lose it."

Her remark instantly reminds me of Paul's letter, when he told me never to let my sparkle die.

"I am so proud of you," she continues. "You are a strong, strong young woman. And you will go so far in life, I know you will."

"Thank you, Mama." I don't push the issue of openin' a shop. I sit and soak in Mama's compliments, and after a moment, I feel proud of myself too.

The next day, Mama ain't up when I'm gettin' ready for school, which is strange, but I hear movement in her room, so I don't bother her.

"See ya later, Mama!" I holler with my mouth full of biscuit and jam, and I head out the door, wrapping my coat tightly around me. I realize I forgot my gloves when I'm halfway down the drive and consider going back for them, but I end up just shoving my hands deep into my pockets. I can handle a little cold. I've handled worse.

The day passes in a whirlwind of holiday activity. The older kids help the younger ones make Christmas ornaments out of popping corn, and then we eat the leftovers, and that devolves into a ridiculous popcorn-throwing match until Miss Glass stomps her boot on the floor and threatens to write letters to all of our parents. Not a single person feels like doing arithmetic, writing, or even reading today – not even Miss Glass, and we soon find out why.

"I'm getting married!" she announces, her face wide with a rosy-cheeked grin. All the kids hop up and down and hug her in excitement, even though the little ones probably don't know what it means to get married. They're just pleased as punch to see Miss Glass so happy, and even more pleased to get to place our attention on somethin' other than school work.

I skip home in the afternoon feelin' like I'm on Cloud Nine. I haven't experienced this amount of joyfulness in a long, long time. Even the sun seems to be smilin'. I sing a hello to JimBoJoe and the hens, and they cluck and chatter in a musical ruckus as I dance up the drive.

I hang my coat up on the hook by the door and holler for Mama. "I'm home. And guess what? Miss Glass is getting married." I don't hear an answer, so I figure she's out back working on her herbs. I trot toward the back porch. "Mama, I'm home."

She's not out there. Oh, she may be in the barn tendin' to Molly. But I would've noticed her as I was comin' up the drive. She coulda taken a walk to see Mrs. Porter down the lane, or even into town to deliver some remedies. Back in the kitchen, I stop and look around. It doesn't look like anything's been touched or moved since I left this morning. Same with the front room. I turn back down the hallway to Mama's room and push open the door. Relief floods me, 'cause there she is, in her bed, and then the relief is followed by fear because Mama would never be in bed at this time in the afternoon.

"Mama, are you alright?" I ask as I move swiftly to her bedside. There's no noise or movement, no tiny snores, no intake of breath, no twitching of covers, no jumping of eyelids in the depths of a dream. I place a hand on her forehead. "Mama?"

Panic sets in and my ears are ringing, my head fuzzy with numbness. "Mama!" I'm shaking her shoulders now, throwing back the covers, and a sob rises up and explodes through my mouth. "Mama, wake up!" I know what's happened, deep down, I know, but there is no way I'm believing it, no way, not today, not now, not ever. "MAMA!"

11

Arrangements

When I wake up, there's a crowd of people. Jimmy, Mrs. Porter, Pastor Klein, Dr. Jamison, Mr. Clay, Mr. Macafee. I'm in my bed, and they're all staring at me.

"Mama!"

Dr. Jamison leans toward me, and I'm out again.

The next time I stir, I hear soothing voices that I haven't heard in a long time. When my eyes gain focus, I see my aunt and uncle and granny. I hear my cousins, but they're not in my room. It's so full of people, no more can fit. Why are they all here?

When I remember, I start to panic, tears forming, and Dr. Jamison leans in again. "No, wait!" I don't want him to sedate me again. "Wait. Please."

Now I'm sobbing. "Is it true?" I plead with all that I have for it not to be. That she was just passed out from exhaustion, or in such a deep sleep I couldn't wake her, or even for the tuberculosis to be back. "Is she—"

Their faces tell me all I need to know, and I turn over and

bury my face in my pillow and cry harder than I've ever, ever cried. It comes from so deep within my soul, like I'm spilling out all of me, all of my life, all of my breath, until I have nothing left inside me.

They're bringing me tea and soup and bread, but I refuse it all. They're asking me questions and rubbing my hands and arms and whispering kind things, but I'm numb and deaf and blind. They're taking turns coming in to check on me, although Jimmy never leaves. I occasionally hear people talking outside of my room. I hear words like *arrangements* and *just a young girl* and *live with family* and *after the burial*.

Suddenly I sit up. I need to see her. "Mama!"

I throw my blanket aside and jump out of bed. Someone calls my name, someone tries to stop me, someone looks at me in shock. "I need to see Mama!"

I push her door open with such force it slams into the wall. I can see she's still in her bed, but someone has pulled her blanket up over her head. Why would they do that? I run to her and pull the blanket down and fold myself over her and sob into her neck.

"Mama, I love you! I love you. You are the strong one. You always were. What will I do without you? I cain't live without you!" And I'm sobbing so hard and holding onto her for dear life, my head buried in her hair, and that's when I notice how cold she is, and I jump back, frightened. I turn around and Jimmy is there, and I fall into him, and he holds me up while I heave more sobs than I knew I had left.

They carry me from Mama's room, and when I look back, someone has pulled the blanket up again, covering her completely, and it kills me to know that's the last time I would ever see her. My mama. My best friend. My teammate. All I had left in the world.

I'm in such pain, that it comes as a shock when I finally recognize that other people are hurting too. My aunt and uncle, my cousins. The people of Maynardville who have known Mama all their lives and who have felt so bad for everything our family has been through. It's at this point that I start thinking of who is to blame.

Dr. Jamison says it may have been heart attack or stroke, but, Lord, she was just fine the day before. She's been in great health, actually, for quite a while. The only thing that's been weighing her down is the grief of losing Josy and Daddy. Heartbreak. So when I search for someone to blame, it don't take me long to land on Paul. He's the one who started it all – all the tragedy in our lives began with Paul Burnett.

During the funeral, I stand away from everyone else. They tried to get me to say a few words and to stand up front, but I've already seen two family members in a pine box; I don't need to see another. Anyway, I'm busy thinking about revenge. I know that's not the Christian thing to think about, and this is not the time and place for thinking such things, but at least it's keeping my mind off of what's happening under the pawpaw trees. The place that used to be me and Josy's favorite spot, where we'd pretend we were on a tropical island. Now it's become an island of death. How'd that happen?

Suddenly we're back in the kitchen, discussing my future. When did the funeral end?

My aunt and uncle want me to come live with them. My cousins would love that, they say. Mrs. Porter says I can stay with her until I finish the school year. Jimmy says I can stay at his house. His mama wouldn't mind 'cause they have an extra room. Next year I'll be seventeen and we can get married, he says. His comment doesn't surprise me, 'cause we've talked about getting married before, but my heart does a little flip before it realizes it's not right to be happy about something right now. Besides, I'm not sure that I'm ready for any of that, and I'm sure not ready for somebody else to plan my life for me.

While everybody's talkin' about what's supposed to happen to me, I'm thinkin' about how I can get away from here and get even with Paul. The only thing stoppin' me is this house, this land, Molly and the chickens, and my whole world out there under the pawpaw trees.

"What will happen to our land?" I ask, looking around at all of the sad eyes, hoping that someone will have an answer.

The men look at one another before Mr. Macafee speaks up. "Well, uh, did your mama have life insurance?"

I laugh at that. Life insurance? Who has the money for that, and anyway, how would I know?

Mr. Macafee looks apologetic and says, "We'll look into that for you, don't you worry, Junebug."

"I don't want to lose the land." I start to cry. "My whole family is buried under the pawpaw trees now." I lower my head into my hands, my shoulders shaking with sobs.

Mr. Macafee and Pastor Klein are both patting my shoulders and back. "It's unimaginable, your losses, June," Pastor Klein says, "and God will provide a way for you to go on. Look to him for help during this tragic time."

I'm quiet for a long time before I turn to Pastor Klein and say, "Pastor, I did look to God. I looked to him when Josy left to ride the rails. I looked to him when we didn't have enough food or money to pay the mortgage. I looked to him when Josy was beat to death by railroad bulls. And I looked to him when Daddy hung himself in our barn. I don't know if I have it in me to look to him anymore." I turn and go to my room and close the door hard enough that everyone knows to stay away.

In the end, we decide that I'll stay with Mr. and Mrs. Porter so I can be close to home, and they'll help me tend to Molly and the chickens. I'll finish the school year, and then … I'll look at my options. If there's life insurance money, I'll be able to keep the land, at least for now. If not – well, I don't know. All I know is that somebody has to pay for me losing my entire family. And it's gonna be Paul.

12

How to Be

I've loaded the wagon with all of my clothes, blankets, books, and everything I want to bring with me to Mr. and Mrs. Porter's farm. I couldn't bring myself to go into Mama's room, not yet, but I folded up her apron and packed it with my clothes. And I found one of Mama's hairpins sittin' on a table in the front room. It won't fit in the tiny marble box, so it's in my hair, and I intend to wear it all the time from now on.

I hitch up Molly and try not to think about why I'm doing these things, packing and loading the wagon. I try to look at it as an adventure, but right now it's impossible to. My stomach feels the dead weight of so much dread. And my head is spinning with questions. What will I do with Mama's things? What about her herb garden? Our furniture? The food in the cellar?

Mrs. Porter told me not to worry about all the little things. She said they'd all work out the way they're supposed to and that I need to focus on the big things. But it's the big things I want to get outa my head so I don't fall completely apart.

Jimmy comes ridin' down the lane on his bicycle, fast enough that he looks like he's in a hurry, but slow enough that he looks like he's afraid to approach me. I understand, 'cause I've been hot and cold with him since ... has it really been a week since Mama's funeral? One week of being completely alone in the world?

Anyway, one minute I'm clinging to Jimmy like he's my savior, and the next minute I want him to leave me alone, and I feel real bad about that, but I cain't figure out how to be right now. How am I supposed to be, without Mama? It was bad enough when I lost my brother and my daddy, and I don't think we'd even figured out how to be without them yet. Now I gotta figure out how to be without them *and* Mama.

Jimmy's been by my side the whole time. On December eighth, when it was Josy's birthday, and I didn't want to leave the house, even though Mr. and Mrs. Porter were beggin' me to come with them right away. When my granny and aunt and uncle and cousins all left and there was an emptiness in the house like you wouldn't imagine. When the hens and the mule needed feedin' and tendin' and I couldn't get outa bed. Finally, this mornin', he said it's time.

"You gotta get outa this house, June," he told me in a gentle but firm voice. "Just 'til school's over. Then we can figure things out."

I knew the Porters were waitin' for me anyhow, and they were so kind to offer to take care of me and the animals. Molly's gonna stay in their barn with their horses, and the chickens will join their brood as soon as we unload my things and come back for them.

When I agreed to get up and start packin', I asked Jimmy if I could be alone for a while. Something about removing my things – and some of Mama's – from the house seemed personal, and I knew I'd need privacy. So he went home to check in with his mama and daddy. Now as he lays his bicycle down and steps toward me, I feel so grateful for him, for his understanding, and for taking care of me so well. I think he's my first true love. I know I once thought I loved Paul, but now I'm sure I didn't. And even if I did, my hatred of him has erased any love that may have been there.

And now I'm thinkin' again about how to make Paul pay for what's happened. This is how I spend most of my time now. It's the only thing that keeps me going. Jimmy climbs into the wagon, and we head down the lane to Mr. and Mrs. Porter's, and we don't talk. He's lookin' at me, just checkin' to make sure I'm okay, I guess, and I'm thinkin' about murder.

Mrs. Porter cooks a big meal, and I gobble it down, 'cause I haven't eaten much in the past few days. Mr. Porter is out in the field with Molly and the horses as the sunlight fades and darkness begins to fall on the farm. Molly fits right in with them, trottin' along and followin' them everywhere like she's a baby again. It's amazing to watch, and I almost smile. Almost.

I think about walkin' down the lane to visit Bug, who's probably cozied up in the barn or curled on the front porch. I know she'll be okay on her own, but I feel bad leavin' her. Then I glance out the window to see the winter wind blowin' the trees around. Maybe I can visit Bug another time.

The Porters' house is cozy and warm, with heavy, flowered curtains hanging over the front room windows. Two lamps light the room with sunny yellow bulbs, and the woodstove sits open, the fiery coals sending out heat and red light. A Christmas tree sits in a corner undecorated. Mrs. Porter says their tradition is to decorate the tree on Christmas Eve.

On my third night here, Mrs. Porter sits beside me on the sofa and places a hand on my knee. "June," she says, hesitating. "There's something I need to ask you."

I nod, unsure what she could possibly be nervous about asking me.

"How would you like to spend this Christmas?"

I think on that a minute, then look her dead in the eye and say, "Mrs. Porter, if you don't mind, I'd like to sleep through it and pretend it isn't happening."

13

I Ain't Takin' No Guff

I get so antsy over the next few days, I can hardly stand it. I remember my conversation with Mama – the last conversation we had – about the herbs and opening up a shop. I remember not understanding how she could be content staying at a standstill. Now I feel like I'm at a standstill.

School's out for Christmas break, I'm tryin' not to break down, and the Porters are walkin' on eggshells tryin' not to break me. I need closure, and the only way to get that is to get on with my plot to get back at Paul. It's now or never, and I'd prefer now.

Before I pack my things and get serious about leaving, I have to talk to Jimmy. I don't know how he'll take it. I'm pretty sure he'll beg me not to go, but I gotta stand strong. This is my battle to fight, and I cain't give in.

On the wagon ride over to Jimmy's, I rehearse what I'm gonna say, but nothin' sounds right, so I keep startin' over.

Jimmy, you know how Paul killed Josy—

Paul is responsible for Josy's death—

The railroad bull that killed Josy cain't get away with it—

When Jimmy comes out to greet me and help me down from the wagon, I take his hands in mine and I blurt out, "I'm going to kill Paul Burnett."

Jimmy does a doubletake and then chuckles like he thinks it's a joke. "What?"

"The railroad bull who killed Josy. I'm going to kill him."

He pulls me onto his front porch, where we can feel the heat from the woodstove inside, and we sit down on a bench.

"June, are you serious?"

"Dead serious."

"What—wait, now, just wait a minute and think this through."

"I have thought it through. I've thought about it for a long time. He beat Josy to death. You shoulda seen the shape he was in when Pate and Charlie brought him home."

"Yeah, but, June, you ain't no killer. You're talkin' about murder here."

"And what do you call what he did to Josy? An accident?"

Jimmy sighs and looks away for a minute, rubbing his palms together. When he looks back at me, there's something in his expression that worries me.

"Look, I know you practically worshipped your brother, but there are things about him you don't know."

I'm taken aback. "What do you mean? What things?"

"Well, I told you about our JimBoJoe days…"

I nod.

"And you asked why we didn't hang out no more, and you asked why I never came to your farm." Jimmy sighs again and stutters.

"Just spit it out," I say. "What are you tryin' to tell me?"

"Well, Joe had a mean streak about him. He started to act

like he was too good for us, and that's why we stopped hanging around each other. And that's why no one in Maynardville would give him any work – he yelled at people, insulted them. His temper was through the roof."

I stand and shake my head. I cain't believe this about Josy. I never seen nothin' like what he's describin', and I lived with him! "What does that even mean, anyhow? Why are you sayin' these things?"

Jimmy stands and reaches for me, but I move back. "I'm just sayin' that whatever happened out there on the railroad … there may have been a reason."

My mouth drops and I feel myself goin' hot and numb. "Are you sayin' Josy deserved what he got?"

Jimmy starts to protest, but I cain't help it, my hand shoots up so fast and slaps him right across the face on its own accord, and I shout at him to go to Hell, and I turn around and stomp down the porch steps and to the wagon, and I cain't get outa here fast enough, and Molly cain't trot fast enough, and I am so furious, the tears and snot are pouring out.

He's callin' my name and runnin' after me, but I get Molly to go faster, and there is no way I'm talkin' to Jimmy ever again. I don't look back, but I can tell when he ain't following me no more, and I'm glad of it. I slow down enough to think about what just happened. Josy had a mean streak? I never seen no such thing. No one in Maynardville would hire him? Maybe that explains why he had to go train hoppin', but that don't mean he did anything to Paul or that he deserved to get beat to death.

More than that, I just cain't believe Jimmy said such a thing. What would possess him to say that about Josy? To *me*?

❦

I write a note for the Porters, tellin' them I'm going to stay with Margaret Ann for a while. I tell them I don't know when I'll be back, and I ask them to take care of Molly for me. I thank them for everything they've done for me these few weeks. Then I grab my pack but stop short of the door and turn around. I go back to the note and scribble, "Merry Christmas."

I've decided I need to go see Margaret Ann first, so at least my note to the Porters ain't entirely dishonest. I have her address tucked away in my pack. The only hobo camp I know how to get to is the one I started my train-hopping adventure at so long ago – out past the big bridge. When I get there, I can ask which train to get on to get to Nashville.

This time around, I don't even bother with a disguise. I got my pistol and a whole lotta anger, and I ain't takin' no guff from anyone, I don't care how tough they are.

Trouble is, I gotta pass right by the road to Jimmy's house, and he's out there waitin' for me. I try to act like I ain't seen him and keep on walkin', but he trots up to me and reaches for my shoulders.

"June, wait, please!"

"Don't touch me, Jimmy."

"Please, let me explain."

I stop and look at him, disbelief in my eyes, and now he looks scared. "There ain't nothin' to explain, other than you bad-mouthin' my dead brother and saying he deserved to die, so I suggest you get outa my way right now, 'cause I got important things to do."

"No, June, I didn't mean that at all." Now he's galloping alongside me as I walk fast down the road. "I just wanted you to know—I just—I don't know, but you can't do this. It's dangerous, and you could get yourself killed. Please, June!"

I ignore him, other than to say, "Well, I'll probably deserve it too," and I keep on walkin'.

I guess that's enough to make him give up, and I'm tryin' not to cry, but my heart is beatin' a mile a minute, and even though I've just started my trek, I feel like I've run a marathon.

It beats even faster when I get to the hobo camp.

14

Lost

I peer through the trees at the camp, which looks the same as the first time – small tents, stools, metal buckets, a firepit – except there's fewer people. I see three men sittin' around the fire, another one sleeping in a lump of coats, and one more leanin' up against a tree. Everybody else is either on a train or inside the tents, and I'm glad of it, because now that I'm here, I'm thinkin' maybe I shoulda cut my hair and dressed like a boy after all. I'm still a teenage girl about to jump on a train with hobos, and I don't know if I'll be safe.

I scoot a little closer, and when a twig crunches beneath my foot, the man leanin' against a tree turns to look. I recognize him. It's Rump, the old toothless man who gave me gloves and showed kindness when I was train-hoppin' on my own. I wish I still had those gloves, but I cain't remember what happened to them. I cautiously step toward him until I'm close enough that I see recognition in his eyes.

"Rump! Do you remember me?"

He nods and says, "You grew ya hair out, boy," and bursts out laughing. I touch my hair, my hand instinctively going to

Mama's hairpin. "Where ya headed?" he asks.

I set my pack down and sit on my legs next to Rump. "I'm goin' to Nashville. To see a friend."

"Just in time, then, young'n. Train comin' up here soon."

I hold my hand out. "You can call me June. It's nice to see you again."

Rump shakes my hand and smiles a jack-o-lantern grin, and the next thing I know, someone's hollerin' that the train is comin'.

This time I do like the men tell me, and I throw my pack up into the train car before grabbin' the bar and jumpin' up. I need to make it look like I know what I'm doin' so's these men will respect me and not try any funny business. Once I get into the car, I scoot to a corner and take my pistol out and stow it in my pants waist so everyone can see I ain't about to be a victim.

There are only six men on this train, and they keep to themselves, settlin' in for a long ride. Two of 'em jump off in Putnam County, somewhere near Cookeville, and it's only then, when the other four are snorin' away, that I allow myself to relax. And I finally feel the bitter cold biting into my skin.

That's when it hits me – I should have brought some of Mama's remedies with me. Why didn't I think of that earlier? Mama concocted a mustard paste with oatmeal that would be useful if I get into some poison ivy. And her ginger root teas cure headaches. Now I'm wishin' I had Mama's whole herb garden in my pocket.

I reach into my hair and pull out her hairpin instead. Tarnished metal with glittery butterfly wings, the pin is small, not gawdy or showy. Dainty, like Mama. I roll it over in my fingers and conjure the image of her wearing it in her auburn hair, always pulled back in a bun or ponytail for her work outdoors or in the kitchen. She rarely let her hair down, but when she did, it swung gorgeously around her shoulders and bounced when she laughed. At least, those are the visions I'm choosing to keep. Instead of the ones of her back when she had the tuberculosis, sick and weak with wilted and stringy locks that needed washing and brushing.

Mama worked hard on keeping the house, the farm, and the family afloat rather than on her appearance. But still she was beautiful.

I blink away the tears threatening to fall and put the hairpin back in my hair. I lean my head back on the hard train car wall and wait. I know I should sleep, but I cain't bring myself to close my eyes again. I don't want to keep seeing all the people I've lost when I close my eyes. It hurts too much.

It's late afternoon by the time we get close enough to Nashville for me to jump. It's cloudy and cool, and the roar of the train weakens to a whisper as it slows to make a curve. That's when I know it's time. I drop my pistol back into my pack and sling the pack over my right shoulder. One of the hobos is already leapin', and I glance back at the rest of the men in the boxcar. The two that are awake are starin' lazily ahead. Must be headin' a lot farther away than I'm goin'.

I look ahead to where I'm jumpin', and there ain't much space between here and the concrete behind a bank of buildings, but I know I gotta hurry. I squat down and lift off, and as I'm jumping, I'm quickly yanked back on the right side, and in a split second, my pack is torn from my shoulder, and I scream out in pain as I tumble to the ground.

I peer up at the train, and there's my pack, snagged on a broken handle, traveling away from me, the top flapping in the wind like it's waving goodbye. *My pack!* I'm huffin' and puffin' from the painful fall, and I'm just about to cry out, when I see the hobo who jumped before me takin' off into some trees around the bend, with policemen chasin' after him. I gotta move.

I drag myself up, rubbing my right shoulder, and I duck in between some buildings. It's a shopping plaza. There are people walkin' along and peekin' into shop windows without a care in the world, as if I didn't just almost get my arm ripped off, as if I didn't just jump off a moving freight train, as if I didn't just lose my mama, and my daddy before that, and my brother before that. I'm dumbfounded as I gape at a family, the mama holdin' a baby in one arm and holdin' the hand of a young'un with the other, the daddy walkin' ten steps ahead of 'em. "Come on, now. Y'all don't hurry up, there'll be nothin' left," he scolds.

My eyes trace their path and find where they're headed. I walk further into the plaza and discover I was dead wrong. These shops people were peeking into ain't even open. They're not walkin' around without a care in the world. They're all headin' to join a line at least a hundred folks deep, and they're waitin' for the day's evening meal.

My mind goes to the food I had in my pack. Now I have nothing. No food, no clothes or blankets, no pistol, and no piece of paper with Margaret Ann's address on it. I sink to the ground and lean up against a lamppost, and I drop my head into my hands and cry in agony.

"Miss. Are you alright?" Three people have stopped to check on me, and I've shrugged them all away with the usual, "I'm fine," but this time I look up because the voice sounds so much like Mama that I almost think it's her come down from Heaven, like God changed his mind and decided I could have her back.

The disappointment must show in my eyes, 'cause the lady

backs up a step and apologizes for botherin' me, and she goes to the end of the food line. I figure I'd better get in that line too, since I ain't got my pack no more, so I walk up behind the lady that sounds like Mama, and I want to hear her talk again, so I ask her what time it is.

"Four-thirty," she says. "The doors open at five-thirty for dinner."

I gape at the long line of people snaking its way to the doors of a church. "Five-thirty!"

"Mmhmm. I usually get here earlier, but…" Then she runs her eyes over me. "Don't you have a coat?"

I realize the jacket I'm wearing ain't much against the December chill, but it hasn't bothered me until now.

"When you get your supper, you can ask for a coat. Shoes, too, if you need 'em."

"Thank you, ma'am." I nod at her and I'm compelled to tell her my whole story for some reason. "I've lost everything."

Her mouth opens slightly as she takes a sharp breath.

"My family, my home … and now—" I choke up and cain't continue.

"You poor thing," she whispers, reaching out but not quite touching me. "I knew something awful must've happened to you. Looks like you've lost all the sparkle from those blue eyes of yours."

I gasp at her comment. For one, because of Paul, and two, because I'd promised myself I would never let my sparkle die. So now I promise to figure out how to get it back. I focus on my mission.

In the hour's wait, I learn that we're in Donelson, just a few miles outside of Nashville, and I have a lot of time to think about how I'm gonna find Margaret Ann. I've written to her enough to remember the name of her street: Wispwood. And

I can almost remember the number – it's either 353A or 535A, or it could be 355. I'm certain there are threes and fives. But never mind that — I definitely remember her phone number. That one magical day that I got to call her on our very own telephone is etched into my brain. NA-five, one-one-three-seven.

Helen, the lady who reminds me so much of Mama that I'm callin' her Mama Helen in my mind, she says there's a telephone in the post office for public use. She gives me a nickel so I can pay to make the call, and I cain't thank her enough. This lady who's standin' an hour in a line to get supper from a church has given me probably her last nickel, and I could just cry.

And I do. Again.

15

By the Light of the December Moon

I don't know how it's possible that an entire year has passed since I came home from those nice folks' farm in Liberty, North Carolina, to find out that Daddy had liberated himself from the pain of living. I never could have imagined what's happened since. If my life were a book, it'd be an epic tragedy, that's for certain.

But over supper with Mama Helen, I'm reminded that I am not alone. She lost her husband and their oldest child in a hunting accident. Now she's raising their three other children the best she can with the help of her ailing mother. I think that must be why there was an immediate connection between us — we've both been through so much, but we're making our way. We're strong women.

After our meal of soup and bread and a small square of cheese, Mama Helen packs up the majority of her food to take home to her children. She wraps my donated coat around me, and we say our goodbyes. I don't tell her who she reminds me of and how I'll never forget her.

As I head toward the post office, carefully following the directions Mama Helen gave me, I'm thinking fondly of her kindness and in some weird way wishing she could come with me.

Her story put things into perspective for me. *We all got our tragedies, June.* That's what Paul had said to me once, after I told him about Josy. And suddenly my sorrow turns to anger. I'm on a mission to kill Paul, and now I no longer have anything to kill him with. It's on a train to Lord-knows-where. I instinctively adjust the butterfly hairpin and say a quick prayer, thankful that I left the tiny marble box with Mr. and Mrs. Porter.

By the time I get to the post office, it's closed, as I shoulda known it would be. It's gettin' dark out now – must be around six-thirty or so. I pull my coat tighter around myself as I think about findin' somewhere to sleep. At the church, they'd offered me a blanket, but foolishly I declined. Don't know what I was thinkin'. I guess I thought I'd be to Margaret Ann's by now and would be curled up under soft comforters by a warm fire.

Around the corner is a small park, and I choose a bench that's under tree cover and sit, wrapping my arms around my knees and wishing I had a blanket. In the distance, over the roofs of the squat buildings, the sun sets in a brilliant show of fiery red and purple.

For the first time since leaving Maynardville, I think about Jimmy, but I don't get angry. I miss him, and I worry that I've made a mistake and lost him forever. I'm not ready to forgive him for what he said, but maybe I overreacted. I think about what he may be doing, and I decide that even if he's furious with me, he's probably lookin' after the house and the land for me. He's probably takin' care of Bug and checkin' in on Molly at the Porters'. But what if he's on a train, tryin' to find me? He would do that, I know he would.

The bowl of soup wasn't enough to fill me up, so pangs of hunger take my mind off of Jimmy. I find things to take my mind off the hunger, like the rumble of car engines on a nearby road, which I ain't real used to hearin'. And the cackle of squirrels chasin' each other around a tree. I get a better look at the shops in the fading light. Some of 'em look like they're just closed for the night, but others look closed for good, with notices posted on their doors and darkness beyond. Those stand out like missing teeth in the row of shops.

It's not until it's totally dark out that I realize I'm not the only one spendin' the night in the park. Just as I'm tryin' to figure out how to get comfortable on this hard bench, I hear a cough comin' from my left. I squint my eyes in the darkness, and by the light of the stars and December moon, I can just make out a lump of a person on another bench. Curious, I look around for more, and I count three more lumps on benches and two up against walls.

I assume these are all homeless folks, unless they just wanna camp out and be first in line for breakfast at the church. I feel a hint of embarrassment to be takin' up a bench that someone who really needs could be usin'. I ain't homeless, after all. Am I?

I didn't really sleep last night. It was far too cold and uncomfortable, not to mention bein' a little scary out here with strangers. So now in the morning light, I'm eager to get goin', but slow goin' at the same time. Besides that, I could use a bath. I hope I can take one at Margaret Ann's house. And get a good meal. Those thoughts light a fire under my feet, and I dart to the post office, only to find that it don't open 'til eight o'clock. Lookin' at the rising sun, I bet it's not even seven yet.

I make the short walk to the church, and there's already folks goin' in and a line forming. I scan the crowd, hoping to see Mama Helen, and I'm disappointed that she's not there. I get a small plate of scrambled eggs and a biscuit, and though it's not as good as Mama used to make, I gobble it down appreciatively. From my spot at the table in the church's narthex, I watch the incoming folks for any sign of Helen. I reach into my pocket to make sure the nickel she gave me is still there, and then I reach for Mama's hairpin in my hair.

I sure could use a mirror. I'm afraid I look a mess. I step around the corner into an alleyway and find a glass door that somewhat shows my reflection. I smooth down my hair and run my fingers through its tangles. I spit on my fingers and wipe my face, then run my finger over my teeth. I stop short of trying to floss with a piece of hair, because that just seems gross, even with clean hair.

When I get back to the post office, the post master is just openin' up the door, and he points me toward a telephone booth in the corner. This telephone's different from the one at home, but the man said it works the same way after I put in the nickel, so here goes nothing.

An operator answers, and my heart is poundin' as I give her the number. I hear the familiar clicks and static and then Margaret Ann's glorious voice.

"I'm in Donelson," I tell her.

"Donelson! Why, that ain't far at all. What are you doin' in Donelson?"

I falter. She doesn't know about Mama, and I don't think I can explain it just now. "I'm comin' to see you."

"Oh, June, that's terrific!" There's a muffled sound and I hear other voices. "Hold on," Margaret Ann says.

When she returns, she asks, "Where exactly are you? My uncle's gonna come get you."

Excitement washes over me. Excitement and sheer relief. "I'm at the Donelson post office, um—" I search until I see the address on the glass door and tell it to Margaret Ann.

"Don't go anywhere, June. We'll be right there!"

I hang up the telephone and feel a smile forming for the first time since Mama died. I thank the postmaster and hurry outside. She didn't say how long it would be, but I don't want to miss her, so here I am sittin' on the curb out in front of the Donelson post office in the middle of winter, waitin' on Margaret Ann's uncle to take me into Nashville. And in Nashville, I'm gonna get a warm bath and a good meal and maybe even a good night's rest before I continue my mission to find and kill Paul Burnett.

16

Joy

When you live on a little ol' farm in a little ol' town, you get used to things that other people don't consider normal. Dust, dirt and mud are always tracked into the house and layer the floor no matter how often you sweep, and boy does it seem like you're constantly sweepin'. Leaves and straw find their way inside and form their own little tumbleweeds in dark corners of the house. Horse flies, spiders, bees, and little "no-see-ums" are practically part of the family. And other critters, like geckos, snakes, mice, squirrels and even the occasional racoon make themselves at home inside, especially when it's too cold outside.

Walkin' into Margaret Ann's house is like walkin' into another world. There's carpet, actual carpet. Wallpaper that's not coated in dust. Plush furniture with pillows and throws. No fly swatter hangin' on a nail in the living room. No broom and dustpan leanin' against the kitchen wall.

They're not rich, Margaret Ann's family, not at all. They're just ... not farm folks. They do things differently, have different lives. I find the differences fascinating, and it takes my mind off of all that I've been through.

Telling Margaret Ann the news about Mama is harder than I thought it would be, to put life to those words, to say them out loud, making them more true, more solid. But I am comforted by the outpouring of love and care from her whole family. It's amazing how a few days and less than two hundred miles can transport me to a life I've longed for since Josy died. A life of joy.

And joy is an understatement. I get to see Say-Lynn and all of Margaret Ann's other sisters and brothers, her aunt and uncle and cousins, and her mama, who dotes on me like nothin' bad ever happened, like she never told Margaret Ann not to be my friend on account of Pate bein' colored and stayin' at our house. And I honestly don't mind none, 'cause she helps me clean up, and she gives me a change of clothes, and she cooks for me, and it's been a long time since I've been taken care of so well, not countin' the Porters.

We're all sittin' around a little kitchen table, squeezed in tight, except for the little ones, who sit on stools by the door 'cause there ain't enough chairs – or space – at the table. Uncle Roger is talkin' about a Christmas parade that's happenin' the next day, and they're all askin' if I can stay for that, and I don't know where my happiness comes from, but it just pours out.

"I'd love to stay!" I practically shout. And just like that, I've forgotten my sorrows and my mission, at least for a little while.

The house is walking distance to a park and shopping center, and even though it's cold, Margaret Ann and I go and explore and gossip and window shop. She shows me the beauty parlor where she does hair, and when we go in and she introduces me to her boss and shows me her station and she's so swollen with pride, I feel thrilled for her. She's really makin' something of herself at only sixteen. Then we go back to Margaret Ann's house, and we spend the rest of the day talkin' and gigglin' and doin' each other's hair.

In the evening after dinner, I get Margaret Ann alone so I can talk to her about my plan, a conversation that I expect will be harder than the one about Mama. But she makes broaching the subject easy, 'cause she asks, "What are you gonna do, June? I mean, now that..."

"Well, I been stayin' with Mr. and Mrs. Porter down the lane, and when I turn seventeen, Jimmy wants to get married." I look up to gauge Margaret Ann's reaction.

"Oh, wow!" Her mouth stays slightly open and her eyes are giant circles.

"But..." My heart and mind are both confused after the fight me and Jimmy had before I left, and I don't really know what's gonna happen.

"But what?"

"He said somethin' awful, and I slapped him."

"Oh, goodness! What'd he say?"

"He said Josy probably deserved what he got, more or less."

"What? No way! Why on earth would he say something like that?"

"He said Josy had a temper and didn't treat people right, so he may have provoked the railroad bulls, which may have led to Paul beatin' him up."

Margaret Ann squints her eyes like she's thinkin' real hard, and then shakes her head.

"He couldn't have meant that, June. I can't imagine Jimmy ever sayin' such a thing."

We sit in silence for a moment before she asks me what I'm gonna do.

"I have a plan, and I know you ain't gonna like it, but it's somethin' I have to do."

She stares at me but doesn't interrupt.

"First I'm gonna go down to Memphis and find Pate. You remember him?"

She nods and looks confused.

"He's the one who witnessed Josy's beating. And he's my friend. I trust him." I take Margaret Ann's hands into mine and lean forward to look deep into her eyes. "I'm gonna find him, and then we're gonna go and make Paul pay for what he's done to my family."

"How're you gonna do that?" Her voice shakes.

"I'm gonna kill him."

Margaret Ann snatches her hands away. "You can't be serious!"

That's exactly what Jimmy had said, and I hope to God my best friend doesn't have the same reaction that he had. "I'm dead serious. He deserves to pay. And if the law cain't do nothin' about his crime, I will."

Now her eyes are full of pity. "You've been through so much. You aren't thinkin' straight. You're not a murderer, June. You're kind and generous and gentle and loving."

I stand up and turn toward the window. "I'm none of those things. Not anymore."

Margaret Ann moves to stand next to me. "There's no way you can get away with this. You just can't."

I whip my head to face her. "And why should Paul get away with beating my brother to death, huh? It's because of him that my daddy killed himself. And because of him that my mama was so heartbroken that she couldn't go on living." I'm too angry to cry now, but I'm breathin' hard and my heart is pounding.

"You have no idea what this is like," I continue, before remembering that her daddy died out on the rails too.

Margaret Ann backs down now, slumping her shoulders, her eyes clouded over like she doesn't recognize me anymore. Maybe she doesn't. I no longer recognize myself.

We get ready for bed in silence. She ain't bein' mean, just withdrawn, and while she's tossin' and turnin' in the bed she shares with her sisters, I sleep like a baby on a pallet on the floor, because I'm just so exhausted.

17

Hopes

The parade the next morning is awash with contradictions. It's a joyous sunny day with blue skies and cheer all up and down Main Street Nashville, but there's a wall up between me and Margaret Ann. Families around us are huddling in tight against the December wind, but me and Margaret Ann stand apart. There's music and big balloons and parade floats, but my heart feels heavy, and I feel like I need to leave, to get back on the train and go to Memphis.

Margaret Ann looks over at me and smiles, an olive branch. I reach out and grab her hand, and we lock fingers, and this is just what I needed. I smile on the inside and out, and by the time Santa Claus comes rumblin' down the road in his sleigh and jingle bells are ringin', me and my best friend are swingin' our hands to and fro' like old times, and our faces wear big ol' grins again.

Back at Margaret Ann's house, she brings me to a small closet in the kitchen, and she pulls out a canvas bag with a long shoulder strap.

"It's not as nice as the one Jimmy gave you, but it should

do." She looks at me for approval, and I nod. Then she moves about the house, finding this and that to put in the bag. A small towel, a bar of soap, toothpaste, some bandages and ointment, a thermos, a small blanket, and two changes of clothes. She looks like she wants to put more in it, but it's almost so full she cain't close and button the flap.

"We'll add food before you leave," she says. "Wh-when are you leaving?"

"Well," I say, uncertainty rising to my chest, "I guess it depends on how long it'll take me to get to the train tracks. You got a map?"

She disappears for a moment and returns with a map, unfolding it on the kitchen table. She points to where we are, just east of the big dot of Nashville. "This don't show the railroads, though," I say in disappointment.

Margaret Ann turns the map over, and there's an enlarged map of Nashville and its surrounding areas. "Here's the train station," she says, and we run our fingers from where we are to the train station. "Does that help?"

I nod. At least if I can find the train station, I'll be able to find the railroad, and it should take me less than an hour to walk to where I need to go.

"What if my uncle drives you?"

"I have to go on my own. It's better this way, I promise."

"Well, we could loan you money for a train ticket to Memphis. It'd be so much safer," Margaret Ann pleads.

I shake my head. "I'd never be able to repay you. Besides, nothin' I'm doin' is safe."

"Exactly," she replies. "This isn't safe. At least let me help you. We can pay for one ticket, I swear we can, and you don't have to pay us back."

I think on that a minute, and it's real tempting. It would

be easy-peasy to ride legally – and comfortably – all the way to Memphis. But if I buy a train ticket, somebody'd be able to track me down. Jimmy and the Porters could find me before I'm able to take care of what I need to do, and I cain't have that. Technically, I'm a runaway, and the Maynardville sheriff's probably searchin' for me already.

"That's dangerous, too," I tell her. "I know you don't understand, but trust me, it's better this way." Since she doesn't look like she's gonna relent, I add, "What you can do is find out for me where the—" I try to think back to the name of the auto shop Pate works at. It was so long ago that he told me, and I wasn't much payin' attention. "I think it's Buddy's or Billy's Auto Shop. In Memphis. I need to find it."

She gets on the telephone with the operator, and in no time, she has an address for me. "There's no Billy's Auto Shop, so it must be Buddy's," she says with confidence, handing me a slip of paper. I fold it and put it into the full bag, which is about to get fuller 'cause now Margaret Ann's handin' me two cans of beans, a can opener, a block of cheese, a roll of sausage, and a bag of rolls. We have to take everything out of the bag and rearrange it to fit the food, but eventually, it's done. When I sling it over my shoulder, it's heavy, and I worry about jumpin' onto a train under this weight. I decide to give her back one of the changes of clothes, which helps only the slightest bit. But once I eat the beans, it'll be lighter.

"I put some money in the inside pocket, for when you need to get more food, okay?"

I start to protest, but she's not havin' it. "Please keep it. It's not much, but I know you'll have use for it."

I realize when I hug her goodbye, it may be the last time I ever see her. For one reason, I might die on this journey; for another reason, I may never make it back to Nashville; and for three, I may end up in prison. So I hug her long and tight, and when I say goodbye to her brothers and sisters, I savor their smiley faces, their freckles, their dimples, and their dirty fingernails and sticky hands. And when I thank her mama and aunt and uncle, I mean it so sincerely, I feel like a grown-up as I use words that seem older than my sixteen years and feel things that only adults should have to feel, like indebtedness and regret.

I leave there praying that Margaret Ann won't tell anyone about my plan and that she won't feel differently about me.

It ain't hard to find the railroad, and I follow it outa town, keepin' my head low and spirits high the best I can. As much as I wish I could navigate this journey on my own, I have to find a hobo camp. I need the hobos to tell me which train to get on, or else I'm liable to end up in Canada or some such place. I wrap my coat tighter around myself, thinkin' this may as well be Canada, it's so cold. Anyway, I know the hobo camps'll be hidden in the woods, so I keep walkin'. I switch my pack from my right shoulder to my left. The loaded bag Margaret Ann gave me is heavier than the pack I left the Porters' with, even without the extra change of clothes, and even without a gun.

I start thinkin' about how I'm gonna get another gun. I doubt anyone would sell me one at a gun store, with me bein' only sixteen and a girl, and I sure don't know where else to get one, 'cept maybe from a hunter, but I don't want no rifle. It needs to be a pistol. Maybe Pate will have a pistol. Yes, Pate will have a pistol, and Pate will get us up to Lafayette, and Pate will help me kill Paul.

I pin all my hopes on Pate, and I keep walkin'.

18

Doin' What We Gotta Do

J ust when I wonder if I'll ever make it to a camp, I hear the tell-tale rumble of a train. I trot toward some stubby trees and brush and duck down as the train approaches and swallows up my breath in its roar. It's goin' at a steady clip, but I spot an open boxcar with men standin' in the doorway.

I run alongside the train under the cover of the small trees and keep my eye on that boxcar. Sure enough, up a ways just before a bend in the tracks, men hop off and roll down the embankment. Now I know where my hobo camp is.

Three things about this hobo camp blow me away when I get to it. First, this is the biggest camp I've seen, and rather than a temporary place to stay while waitin' for the next opportunity, this one seems more ... permanent. It looks like they done built themselves a house here in the woods alongside the railroad. Outa real wood and even some bricks. Clotheslines string their way between the building and trees, sagging under the weight of so many britches and coats. A makeshift oven leans next to a firepit, and a pond beyond appears to offer baths, dishwashing, and recreation all at once.

I count at least five residences stretched out in a row beyond the wooden structure that must be a common kitchen and I-don't-know-what-all else, and through a tiny trail deeper into the woods, I spot an outhouse. I wonder about the folks who live here and whether they'll run me off or let me stay 'til the train to Memphis comes.

All the folks are gathered around the open porch of the kitchen house, and this is the second amazing thing: They're havin' a church service, with a preacher and everything. How I can tell it's a church service is that the preacher man is standin' and holdin' his arms out like he's blessin' everybody, and everybody else is kneelin' right there in the dirt with their heads bowed. I can hear the voice of the preacher man, but I cain't make out what he's sayin', until what must be the end of his prayer, and he says, "A blessed Christmas to you all," and the people start singing *O' Holy Night.*

Of course! It's Christmas. How remarkable that I forgot about Christmas. I'd told Mrs. Porter that I wanted to sleep through it, but now that it's here, I feel guilty for some reason, like by ignoring Christmas, I'm betraying the people I love. I steady myself against a tree and bow my head, praying for Mama and Daddy and Josy, and I apologize to Jesus for not wantin' to celebrate his birthday.

When I look up, the song has ended, and folks are gettin' up and movin' about, and that's when I see the third thing that blows my mind. Sittin' on the edge of the group is a woman and two children, one on her lap, and one to her side. This is the first time I've seen a woman at a hobo camp, and the first time I've seen little kids at one, too. The woman's wearing a weather-beaten dress and a wool sweater, and she's sharing a large blanket with her kids, all wrapped up and huddling together. Then I notice that the hand that ain't holdin' the blanket over her kids is holdin' a long rifle.

As I'm gazing at this woman, I realize that she sees me staring at her, and I don't know if it's just my imagination, but I think I see her grip tighten on her gun. I move out of the shadow of the tree and step toward the woman. There's an overturned crate next to her, and I point to it and raise my eyebrows. She eyes me warily, but doesn't say no, so I sit, lowering my pack to the ground between my feet.

"I'm June," I say, trying to sound nice and cheerful without bein' loud enough to draw attention to us. "Merry Christmas."

"Same to you," she says, unsmiling. I notice she didn't offer a name.

"I'm from Maynardville." I get no response, and she draws her children in closer.

After an awkward silence, I try again. "Where you headed?"

The woman squints her eyes at me. "Look, we ain't here to make friends. Just to make do. So run along."

I drop my mouth. And as I sit here gaping at this woman, the anger begins to boil inside me. *Run along?* How insulting. She clearly doesn't have the motherly instinct of helping someone in need. Who would turn away a child like that? I mean, I am still a child, just sixteen, and all alone.

She was looking straight ahead like she was tryin' not to see me, but now she glares at me, so I hold my hands up and inch back on the crate.

"I'm just tryin' to make do too," I tell her. "I lost my whole family. Ain't got nothin' left, so all's I need is to know which train goes to Memphis."

Even though I know I'm stayin' right here whether she

wants me to or not 'cause I feel safe next to this woman with her rifle, I pretend like I'm gettin' up to leave, and she says, her voice low, "It'll be the West Tennessee line. Big, red steamer."

"Thank you." I relax my shoulders. "Anybody know when?"

She nods toward the preacher man. "Henry knows."

I learn that Henry is pretty much the leader here, even though he's one of the youngest men. Maybe that's why he's the leader – still got his strength and sense. Anyway, he knows the lines, the trains, the times, and everything. Plus, he gives sermons and blessings. Now I know that I gotta get on the red train tonight, and just about everybody here is doin' the same. Everybody wants to go to Memphis, including the woman and her children.

"How old are your kids?" I think tellin' me about Henry was her way of accepting me, but I don't know if she's gonna talk to me any further. And just when I'm sure she's ignoring my question, she speaks.

"Little one's five, littler one's eighteen months."

"And they jump on trains with you? Moving trains?"

Her eyes shoot daggers at me, like I've insulted her parenting.

"I didn't mean nothin' by that—"

"You think I don't know it's dangerous? Livin' on the streets of Nashville is more dangerous. Stayin' in a house with a drunkard is more dangerous. I'm doin' what I gotta do, and in case you ain't noticed, I got plenty of protection for me and my kids," she says, and she swings the top of the rifle in front of her. "Anyway, you're just a kid yourself, so what would you know about it?"

Her kids are staring at me like they'd jump up and fight me if their mama asked them to, even though they ain't but little ol' wisps.

"That rifle you're hangin' onto is why I sat next to you in the first place. I shoulda disguised myself as a boy again, but I thought my gun was protection enough. Now it's gone. And so's my whole family, so ... I'm doin' what I gotta do too."

There's a long silence between us as we listen to the chatter of others in the camp.

"I'm Mary," the woman says finally. "You got somethin' to eat?"

19

Sparkle

Henry the preacher man wakes us about twenty minutes before the train to Memphis is due to come by. More than half the camp is packed up and ready to go in no time, and we quietly hike toward the bend in the railroad, where the train will have to slow down. Henry leads us with a dim flashlight, and then we all crouch down in the tall weeds.

When the train rumbles near, Henry and another man summon me and Mary to the front. He turns off his flashlight, and I wonder how we're gonna be able to see to get on the train, it's so pitch black. Then the train approaches, slowly, and I see light coming from the steam engine, and it's enough to guide us to the boxcars.

The other man jumps effortlessly on and holds his hand out to Mary, who has the baby wrapped around her. The man pulls her up as Henry gives her a lift from the ground and then quickly lifts up the other child for Mary to grab, and in a matter of seconds, Mary and her kids are safely onboard. It's a well-oiled machine, the way they work together. They make it look easy.

Henry pushes me toward the train, and I run to catch up with Mary's boxcar, grab the handle and swing my legs up. Once I'm in, I look down to see all the other men runnin' and jumpin', and I quickly scoot in to sit next to Mary. Henry doesn't get on.

"He lives in Nashville," she says.

"At the camp?"

"No, I think he has an apartment downtown."

"He what?" I'm shocked as a cow caught in barbed wire. "He ain't a hobo?"

She grunts, and I wonder if that's her version of a laugh. "Well, that's a matter of opinion, but, no, he don't live at the camp, and no, he don't jump trains."

"So he gives sermons and hangs around the hobo camp for fun?"

"He helps, is all. He's a preacher. Ain't that what preachers do?"

Mary's kids start to whine, and she says it'll be a few hours 'til we get to Memphis, so we should go back to sleep. From her pack, she unrolls her blanket and tucks her kids into it on the floor, and it seems like they're out like a light in a split second.

I put the soft hood of my coat up over my head and lay down, using my lumpy pack as a pillow, and think about Henry helpin' all the hobos at the camp but not bein' a hobo himself. I look up at Mary, who's still sittin' up against the wall of the boxcar with her long rifle across her lap.

"Ain't you gonna sleep?" I ask her.

"I gotta keep watch."

I turn my head and only just now realize how crowded the train car is. By the light of someone's lantern, I can see hobos lining every inch of the inside walls. Some of 'em curled up on the floor, some of 'em sittin' with their backs against the wall like Mary. And some of 'em starin' right at us. A shiver runs through me, and it ain't 'cause I'm cold, and suddenly I wish Henry were here with us. But I look back at Mary, who's starin' right back at them men. There's no fear on her face, no sir. And because of her, I'm able to fall asleep.

What seems like only a few minutes later, I'm bein' shaken awake. It's still dark, and I'm guessin' it's about one or two o'clock in the morning.

"There's a friendly farm on the way to the Memphis camp," Mary whispers. "They leave jugs of water and packets of food in a big box on the edge of their property for us."

"Like a Memphis welcome wagon!"

I wonder how Mary's gonna jump off the train with her little ones without Henry here to help. I'm about to ask what I can do – I picture her tossing the baby to me once I'm on the ground – but I feel the train slowin' down almost to a stop. Mary hops off with the baby in her arms, then trots alongside the train and grabs the older one's hand and swings him down like it ain't nothin'. I'm so amazed by it that I almost forget to jump down myself.

Dark dust kicks up beneath the boots of all the men hoppin' off the train, and I catch up to Mary, who has separated herself from the group of hobos and is holding her blanket up, stretched out in her hands like a curtain.

"What are you—" Oh. Her babies are relievin' themselves, and suddenly I realize I haven't done so myself in I-don't-know-how-long. So once they're done, me and Mary take turns holdin' the blanket up for each other, the shufflin' of boots and low hum of the hobos gettin' farther and farther away.

It's slim pickings when we get to the box of goodies left by the friendly farm folks, but I'm glad the hobos left us something. We fill our canteens up with water, and we grab some rolls, a few pieces of bacon wrapped in tinfoil, two containers of soup, and I'll be darned! There's a handful of caramel cubes! I cain't believe it.

"Well, you sure look like you got your sparkle back," Mary says, and I'm so excited about the caramel cubes that I hardly even shudder at her words. Hardly even think about how it must be some kinda sign that people keep talkin' to me about sparkle when they don't know the story. Hardly even wonder what in the world the universe is tryin' to tell me.

20

Finding Pate

First thing in the morning, I pack up and look over the auto shop address Margaret Ann gave me. Mary's sittin' against a tree, still guarding her little ones. She didn't ask me and probably don't care, but I tell her anyway: "I'm headin' out now."

All she does is nod.

"Thank you, Mary, for watchin' after me even though you got your own young'uns to watch after."

And Mary does somethin' I ain't seen her do yet. She smiles. "You be safe, now," she says, and I leave there hopin' I'll see her again next time I get on a train.

I have no idea how I'm gonna find this auto shop. All's I know is, I gotta head west toward the river, and the further I walk, the bigger everything looks – buildings, streets, signs, and cars. Ain't many people out and about this early on a— *crumbs!* I don't even know what day it is.

Up ahead, I see a smartly dressed couple gettin' outa their car. I speed up to catch 'em.

"Excuse me," I holler. "I need to find this address." I hold the paper out to them and the man takes it to look at it up close.

He squints his eyes at me before handing the paper back and shakin' his head. "You got no business hangin' around that neighborhood, young lady."

"It's important. I have to find somebody."

I guess the woman feels sorry for me, 'cause she says to her husband loud enough for me to hear, "This early in the mornin' shouldn't be any problem."

The man stuffs his hands in his pants pockets, jingles keys or coins or something, and finally says, "I doubt you'll find any of your people over there, but ..." then he points with his whole hand, not just a finger, "you'll need to head a little further south. Follow Beale street, and then get on over to your left when you're closer to the river."

"Thank you, thank you, thank you!" I run off but can hear them shoutin' for me to be careful. I got no earthly idea why they're so worried – they don't even know me. How do they think they know what kinda people I'm lookin' for?

I'm ecstatic when I find Beale Street. And amazed. I remember when Paul took me to see Roanoke and how thrilled I was to see all them tall buildings and hotels and theater. Well, Memphis got Roanoke beat, that's for sure. Everywhere I look, there are restaurants and buildings with flashy signs that look like they light up, but ain't nothin' open yet.

One building I come upon has a sign on the front window, and I step closer to read it. *Big Jitterbug Contest. $30 in cash. Colored Citizens Club.* I look up at a hotel sign and notice it says *Best Colored-Only Service.* And suddenly I know what that couple meant. Do I belong here? Will I get in trouble? I scoot under an awning and into a shadowed corner and scan the area. I see a couple of cars parked along the street, and I see and hear some signs of movement in some of the shops, but I don't feel like I'm in danger. I wish I knew what time it was.

And just as if God heard my wish, a clock is hangin' onto a building when I round the corner. Glad I can read Roman numerals, I see that it's a little after seven. I head left, like the man told me, and then turn to walk parallel to Beale Street.

This street is narrower, more closed in, and lots of the buildings look closed down. But as I keep walkin', I can hear the clangin' of tools and engine noises, and I know I must be almost there. Then, just as I round a curve in the road, I see it. Buddy's Auto Repair. There's an open garage with a couple of cars in it, and there are four or five men that I can see – all colored.

I wonder if they're gonna chase me off, but I ain't scared. I just ain't used to it, bein' from a little farm in Maynardville. I let out a chuckle 'cause I think about Margaret Ann's mama, and Lord, wouldn't she have a fit!

I walk up to the nearest man, who's in the open doorway of the garage, and when I clear my throat and he turns around, he looks at me like I got horns growin' outa my head.

"Um…" I look at the nametag on his overalls. "Hello, Mr. Aaron. I'm lookin' for an old friend of mine named Pate," and while I'm waitin' for Aaron to answer me, I look around at the other workers in the garage, and they're all starin' at me, but none of 'em are Pate. "Does he work here?"

He turns to the others. "Fellas, this young lady here wants to see Pate." A couple of them laugh, and someone says, "Is that right, now?" like they're all suspicious or somethin'. Or they're playin' games with me.

Then Aaron turns back to me. "What would a nice girl like you want with an old colored boy?"

I ain't sure how to answer that. "Like I said, he's my

friend. And how do you know I'm nice, anyway?"

"Pate ain't got no white friends, and he sure as hell ain't got no white girlfriend. Now you run on along."

In an instant, I'm fuming. Why do people keep tellin' me to run along? I push up closer to him and stand on my tiptoes, and that's when I realize short little ol' me is just about as tall as this man here, and standin' on my tiptoes almost lets me look him square in the eye.

"You listen here," I spit out, a fierceness in my voice that I only ever remember hearin' that time on the train when I pointed my gun at the men who were beatin' Pate to a pulp. "Pate took care of my brother when they was hoppin' trains, and then he took care of me when I was hoppin' trains all by myself. Now I need to see him, and I'm gonna see him whether you like it or not. So if he's here, go get him. If he's not here, I'll wait." And I cross my arms and scowl at him, tryin' not to let him see me shakin' in my boots.

"P-please," I add, so as not to be too disrespectful.

I notice some of the others shakin' their heads and smilin' and gettin' back to their work. The opponent in front of me backs up a smidge, squints at me, then finally lets out a laugh. "Pate ain't workin' today," he says. "Come back tomorrow."

I decide to push my luck. "Where can I find him right now?"

"Listen, little girl, I ain't about to give you my worker's address, so like I said, run along and come back tomorrow."

I cross my arms tighter and plant my feet. "I'll ... I'll camp out here. I could probably sleep in one of them cars over there."

Poor Aaron looks like he got no idea what to do with me.

It wasn't hard for me to find the apartments, 'cause good ol' Aaron gave me exact directions, but the few folks I passed by on the way looked at me like they don't want me here. Now I don't know what I'll find when I walk up the steps to apartment 210 and knock on the door.

Aaron had said Pate lives here with a few of his friends. I wonder if they're all awake. It's still early in the mornin'. I take a deep breath and knock quietly so's I don't anger anybody by wakin' them up. But what if they didn't hear the knock? And if I don't wake anybody up, how will they come to the door? I wait a minute and debate knockin' again. Maybe this time I'll do it a little bit harder.

Right when I'm about to knock again, the door opens just a smidge, the chain lock clinking as it's stretched to its limit. All's I can see is one eye, a nose, and part of a mouth pokin' through the sliver of space, and I'm pretty sure it ain't Pate.

"Whatchu want?" the mouth asks.

"I'm—I'm looking for P-Pate," I manage to shake out.

The eye, nose, and mouth retreat from the space and the door closes. I wonder whether the person just shut me out or is going to get him or what. I hear the chain slide in its socket and the door opens again.

Pate steps out. At least, it kinda looks like Pate, except he's got hair on his face and he looks older than I remember. I look for that kind twinkle in his eyes like I saw when I first met him, and it's there. Barely, but it's there, so I smile.

"Pate! Do you remember me?"

"June, what—"

He grabs my arm and pulls me down the stairs. "You can't

be here. What are you doin'?"

"Well, it's good to see you too."

He suppresses a smile and leads me around a corner into a narrow alley. "It is good to see you, it really is." He looks at me for a minute, then says, "Man, it's been a long time. You all grown up. You look just like your brother."

Before I can respond, he turns all hard and scolds, "But I'm serious, you can't be seen here."

"Why not? It's a free country."

Pate shakes his head. "You ain't changed one bit, have you? It's dangerous."

"Well, I ain't seen nothin' dangerous yet."

"That's 'cause it ain't even eight o'clock in the mornin' yet," he says. "Why'd you come here lookin' for me? And how'd you find me, anyhow?"

"Aaron gave me directions."

"Aaron did? Really?"

"Well, I had to threaten him, but, he eventually spilled."

"Wait—you *threatened* my boss? With what?"

"I threatened to camp out there at the shop to wait for you."

Pate laughs a hearty laugh, shakin' his head. "Girl, you … I can't believe you did that. You are just like your brother, you know that? Son of a gun."

And he keeps shakin' his head, and once he's finally done laughin', he asks again, "So why'd you come lookin' for me?"

I hesitate, a lump growin' in my throat, and he must see the pain in my eyes, 'cause he says, "What happened?"

"Mama died."

There's a long silence, and I can see the minute he makes the realization that I've now lost everyone in my family. His eyes go so dark with empathy that I feel bad for tellin' him. He looks like he might cry.

"Oh, Lord, June, I... I don't know what to say, that's so..." and he's shakin' his head, and I understand. I've seen so many people at a loss for words. I don't even know what I would say if it were the other way around and Pate were tellin' me his whole family was gone. So I know how uncomfortable it is for folks. I figure I'd better tell him my plan.

"The reason I'm here is..." except I ain't so sure how to put it. "Well ... you remember Paul, the railroad bull that killed Josy? He has to pay for what he done, and I believe now is the right time to make him pay."

As I say this, Pate's eyes are getting wider and wider, and I'm afraid I'm about to get another earful of exactly what Jimmy and Margaret Ann said when I told them, so I speed my talkin' up and raise my voice and my hand. "Now, I know it must sound crazy to you, but dang it, he killed Josy, and because of that, my daddy killed hisself, and because of that, my mama died of a broken heart, and I ain't about to let Paul get away with all that."

Pate stops me, his eyes dark again. "Wait a minute. You never told me that's how your dad—"

"I know," I gulp down a sob that wants to come out. "I'm sorry. I don't know why I didn't tell you that day you came by, I just... I guess I didn't want you to think poorly of him."

"I don't. I won't." He looks down, hands in his pockets, and we're quiet for a bit again.

"So will you help me?"

Pate looks up, astonishment in his eyes. "What are you talkin' about?"

"I'm gonna go up to Virginia." I lower my voice to a whisper. "And I'm gonna kill Paul."

At the same time that Pate starts protesting and thrashin'

his arms around and pacing and shakin' his head, I'm tryin' to get him to listen. "I brought my pistol, but I lost it on a train, so I gotta make a new plan, figure out how else I can kill him, or where I can get a gun, but that's where you come in. At least, that's where I was hopin' you'd help. I want us to do it together. Will you come with me?"

He runs his hand down his face, and he looks furious. "No, June, no, no, no, you ain't gonna go to no Virginia, and you ain't gonna kill nobody."

Immediately, I'm pleading. "I have to! And I'm tired of explainin' this and people not understanding. It's simple. He's responsible for my whole family bein' gone, so I want him gone. And I'm gonna do it with or without your help, but it'd be easier with it, so you might as well come with me."

Now he's got tears in his eyes. "I can't. I can't come with you."

"Why not? Cain't you take a couple of days off work?"

"It ain't about work."

"Then what?"

Now his face is red. "Girl, where you been livin'? We in the South. Folks don't like to see people like me with people like you. It could get us killed. Both of us."

It's my turn to be astonished, 'cause I never heard of such a thing. I mean, I know some people are nasty to colored folks, but this don't make a lick of sense.

"Listen," he says, his voice sad and weary. "I need to tell you somethin'… about the day Joseph was beat up—"

"By Paul," I interrupt.

"That ain't the point, just listen. When the bulls got ahold of us, one of 'em was knockin' me around, and Joseph stood up for me. Them bulls didn't like that. They called him names. They let go of me and went after him worse, but he didn't back down."

I can hardly breathe.

"I think he got it worse because of me. Because he defended a colored boy." Pate reaches for my hands but then draws back, like he's afraid. "I don't want that to happen to you."

21

I Choose the Train

My mind travels back to the night Pate told me it was Paul who beat up Josy. How it was so hard to believe him, and I was so confused. I feel that way now.

"How come you never told me?"

"I guess the same reason you never told me 'bout your daddy."

We walk down to the river and wind our way into a thicket of trees, silent mostly. Taking in all that we've learned today. It weighs heavily on both of us.

"It wasn't your fault, Pate," I say, my whisper loud among the quiet morning river sounds.

He nods, but his eyes say, *Yes, it was.*

"Paul's to blame here, and only Paul. And he needs to pay for it."

After another moment of silence, Pate says, "I know where you can get a gun."

And that's how Pate can help me, it turns out. He cain't come with me, no matter how hard I try to persuade him, but he can point me in the direction of a gun.

"But listen here, June," he says, all serious-like. "If you change your mind, that's okay too. 'Cause Paul will get what's comin' to him. You ain't gotta get involved."

"I know."

"And you keep yourself safe."

I nod, my eyes filling up. For some reason, this feels like a permanent goodbye, and I don't like it.

"Pate, I'll see you again," I say, convincing myself as well as him. "Real soon. You'll see."

But I don't turn around when I head back up to the street.

I use all the money Margaret Ann gave me and buy a tiny pistol offa some kid in a back alley. He charged me extra for some bullets. "I'll only need one," I told him, but I took six anyway.

I keep my new gun hidden in my pack and won't take it out until I get on a train (Pate's orders), and before long, I'm outa Memphis proper and comin' up to a hobo camp. I'm disappointed that I don't see Mary and her kids, but she's probably found herself some work. Maybe she'll come to the camp later. In the meantime, I need to eat and wash up.

I've always wondered what hobos and train hoppers do when it rains, wondered how they survive. Well, this is the day I get to find out, 'cause right after I eat a can of beans (yep, I eat the whole can of "magical fruit," and because I'm a lady, I will not mention what them beans are making me do), thunder rumbles (louder than my stomach) and the rain comes down in sheets. I guess that's my washin' up. The camp is tucked into some thick woods and brush, so the trees provide some cover, but in a rain like this, that ain't enough.

We all gather around the largest tent, some squeezed in like sardines and others hunkering down under an awning, and it would almost be better to suck it up and sit out under the trees. Almost. It's freezin' cold 'cause of the rain, and my coat's gettin' soaked, and I feel like cryin'. But I don't, 'cause everybody else seems cool as a cucumber. I guess they're used to this and know how to handle it.

When the rain starts comin' down harder, somebody produces a tarp and holds it up over our heads since the rain's comin' in sideways. It reminds me of the time it rained so hard on my twelfth birthday, and it was Sunday, so we were goin' to church even though it was pourin' cats and dogs. We had a little ol' tarp to hold over us in the wagon, but we got soaked anyway, 'cause the wagon got stuck in the mud, and Daddy and Josy had to try to pry it loose, and then we ran, slippin' and slidin', to the front porch. I remember Mama's deep laugh gurgling out when we collapsed in a heap, and Daddy couldn't figure out what in the world could be so funny.

The only difference now is that it's late December, and the rain is colder than a confused coonhound's nose. I shiver in my drenched coat and hug my knees to my chest as rain drops pour down my face like tears. The canvas bag Margaret Ann gave me is no protection against the downpour, and I know everything inside it is sopping wet. I can feel mud and water seepin' into my britches as the campsite turns into a swamp. And even though it's mid-afternoon, it's dark gray and gloomy.

There's a clap of thunder, and in the momentary flash of light, I see a hobo sittin' across from me, starin' at me so hard I have to look away. Now, every so often, my eyes turn back to his direction without me even tellin' 'em to, just to see if he's still starin'. And he is. Every single time.

"We have to move to higher ground!" someone shouts over the roar of the rain. "Creek's floodin'."

The camp-turned-swamp has now become a rushing stream. I jump up, and everybody's gatherin' their things and runnin', so I follow them. We climb up a rocky hill, slippin' in the mud, grasping at shrubbery and tree limbs. Someone grabs ahold of my arm, and I look back, and it's the man who was starin' at me. I shake him off and move faster.

Just as we get to the top of the hill, I look down and watch the angry waters wash the tent away. The tent that we were huddled under only minutes ago.

It's still rainin' steadily when I hear the telltale noises of a train in the distance. I look at the folks sittin' nearest me, and they don't look like they're gettin' ready to go nowhere.

"There's a train," I say.

"Cain't jump in the rain," one man says. "Too dangerous."

I look around and notice a couple of hobos headin' down toward the tracks. "They're going," I say to the man, as some sort of proof that it can be done.

"Yeah, they'll be lucky to survive. Too slippery."

I think on that a minute, and I come to agree that it'd be mighty hard to grab a slick, wet handle, and anywhere I plant my feet on the jump would be slippery. I'd be liable to fall.

But then I spot the creepy man from before. Now he's peekin' out from behind a tree, still starin' at me with a grin on his face. I gotta get outa here. Do I risk jumpin' and fallin' from a wet train in the rain, or do I take my chances here at this hobo camp with a strange man who's got his eyes on me for some reason or 'nother?

I choose the train.

22

Accident

I sling my bag over my head and shoulder and try to catch up to the men who already left for the tracks. The stream ain't rushin' through the original camp no more, but it's one big, swampy puddle. I'm lookin' for ways to cross it when I spot the men, who are shufflin' along a downed tree. I make my way toward them, trudging through sludge and thorns, and me and my bag are weighted down with so much water that it's hard to move. But I ain't got time right now to wring everything out. Besides, it's still rainin', so the minute I squeeze water from somethin', it'll fill right back up again. I'll just have to do the best I can.

Funny thing about water: You either don't have enough or you got too much. Ain't no middle ground, for some reason. I guess that's the way life is with everything. Nothin' can be just right. Nothin' can be perfect. But I promise myself that I won't let my mind spiral down that dark hole. I got a gun and I'm on my way to make Paul pay for ruinin' my life. That's close enough to perfect for now.

I catch up to the two men after crossing the tree bridge, and I follow them down to the tracks, the noise of the train gettin' louder. When they see me behind them, they beckon me over.

"You ever jumped in the rain?" one of 'em asks.

I shake my head, my lips clamped shut so's I don't say somethin' wrong.

He looks at my hands. "Where're your gloves?"

I shake my head again, wishin' I still had the ones Rump gave me a year ago.

He turns to the other man and holds out his hand. "Glenn, gimme those extra gloves you got." Meanwhile the train's gettin' closer.

"Quick. Put these on," he says, handing me the gloves. They're way too big, no surprise.

The man shakes his head. "Naw, that ain't gonna work," he spits. Then he snatches the gloves off my hands, reaches into a side pocket of his pack, and pulls out a knife.

I'm wonderin' if I need to run the other way when he kneels next to a tree stump and starts cuttin' the ends of the fingers off the gloves.

"Hurry, Dan," the man named Glenn says. *Dan. Short for Daniel.* I may be goin' crazy, but I feel like it's destiny that this man is helpin' me, seein' as how he has the same name as my daddy.

When he's finished cuttin', I stick my hands out, and Dan tugs the gloves tightly onto my hands and uses some kinda cord to tie them at the wrist.

"There, that'll help your grip. Now lemme see the bottom of your boots."

I lift one foot, and he explains how to plant my boot on the edge of the open boxcar floor for the most stable contact.

Then I gotta swing up quick, before I go slidin'. He also says I have to throw my pack in first, and before he's done explainin', the train is upon us, and we're runnin' alongside it in the rain, and I'm prayin' that I can make the jump.

Glenn and Dan jump first, and I watch them. These hobos have probably jumped a million times, and it looks like it's a struggle for them, hands and boots slippin', curses comin' out of their mouths. But once they're in, they motion for me, and I throw my pack in. Outa the corner of my eye, I sense other folks comin' toward the tracks, but I try to stay focused on the task in front of me: Grab the handle, plant my boot, don't die.

I'm winded once I've thrown myself into the boxcar. Winded, heart pounding, but alive. I grab my pack and smile at Dan. I'm about to thank him, but he pushes me outa the way just as another hobo leaps up into the car, and another, and then two more. I back into a corner, and my heart sinks when I see that the creepy staring man is one of 'em.

The others are chattin' and settin' out their mats and tarps to sit on, dryin' themselves off the best they can with towels and blankets. Washin' up and dryin' off has completely left my mind as I keep an eye on the creepy man. I dig my gun out of my pack and tuck it in my waistband, making sure he sees I've got it. I keep my hand on it to send a message, and I don't look away when he gazes at me with dark, evil eyes.

Somebody opens up a can of ham, and the smell of it fills the whole train car, reminding me that I haven't eaten anything since before the storm. I take my hand off my gun for just a minute to find somethin' to eat in my pack. That was a mistake.

The creepy man lunges for me, grasping at my waist, my hips. I use my knees, kicking him where I can, and I get to my feet and move across the car. He comes after me, again grabbing for my waist and trying to pin my hands behind my back. I'm so frightened, I'm nearly paralyzed by the idea of what I think he aims to do.

It's not 'til someone shouts, "Get offa her! You cain't have her gun. Go back to your whiskey, now, Barney," that I realize he's not after me – he's after my gun, and even though I'm still stuck in a dangerous situation, I'm so relieved, I ain't even gonna lie about that. I find myself smiling and gaining confidence, now that I know he's a drunkard, too.

I slam the heels of my hands against the front of his shoulders, knockin' him back a little. He's a wiry man, not very strong, but he lunges for me again. Now we're edging toward the open side of the car, and he wraps his body around me like a prize fighter who's beat up and tired. I smell his stench and alcohol, and his greasy hair is in my face. In my disgust, I thrust forward and thrash my body side to side to shake him off.

"Get offa me!" I give a final push, and what happens next goes in slow motion. His eyes are open wide, and his arms flail up and back as he slips on a slick wet spot at the edge of the car. My hands go up to my face as I take in a gulp of air and hold it there. The man is still falling, off balance, and he bumps into the wall and spins around and then he's plummeting out the open door of the boxcar.

"No, noooo!" I reach out, but it's too late. He's fallen, and we hear a stilted scream and then the bump-bump-bump of his body rolling under the train, and I'm screaming now.

"I've killed him. I've killed him. Oh my God, I've killed him!" I'm hysterical, and now Dan is by my side, and he's pulling me back to the safe side of the car, but I cain't breathe, I cain't breathe, I cain't breathe.

I sit with my arms around my knees, and I rock back and forth, and my mind keeps replaying the image of the man tumbling off the train. "I didn't mean to," I cry. "I didn't mean to, I didn't mean to."

Dan pats my arm. His friend Glenn is on my other side, and some of the other men have scooted closer and are watchin' me. "I know you didn't," Dan says. "We all know that. We saw what happened."

"That ol' Barney was bad news," somebody says. "Think that was his name, Barney."

"A no-good drunk," someone else says.

"He was attacking you, and that ain't right," Dan says, but I just cain't believe what's happened, and no matter how much they try to convince me that I ain't done nothin' wrong, I know I've just killed a man. *I've just killed a man.* I put my arms across my knees and lay my head into my arms and sob.

23

Barney

My eyes are red and sore, my stomach aches, my head is filled with terrifying visions and thoughts. My first thought is that I want to go home. But I remember that Mama's not there for me to go home to, and that sends me into more crying and panic. My second thought is that I need Jimmy. But then I remember that I slapped him and shouted at him and left him in an angry state, so I don't have him to go home to no more, either. More crying and panic.

So I have a third thought – the Porters. I can go home to them, and they'll take care of me. But that thought doesn't sustain me. They're nice and all, but they ain't family, not really.

The fourth thought I have is the one that breaks me: I cain't kill Paul. I just killed a man on accident – a bad man, at that – and I'm devastated. How can I kill a man on purpose, no matter what he's done to me or my family? And if I cain't kill Paul, then what am I doing? What is this all for?

I have no answers. I feel like I have no purpose in life now. Nothin' to do and nothin' to live for and nowhere to go. I hunch over in the corner of the train car, make myself small, and cry myself to sleep.

When the train is nearing a train yard in Nashville, Dan nudges me awake and says we need to jump off and hide while this train loads up and another one unloads. Nashville. Feels like I was just here.

I let Dan and Glenn practically carry me off the train and to a hobo camp. It's the same one where I met Mary and her kids, but it's dark now, so I cain't tell if they're here. I don't think I can face them, anyhow, after what I done. I don't think I can face anybody.

Dan and Glenn set up a tent that has an awning, and they roll out a sleepin' bag under the awning for me to use. I lay my bones down and I feel so heavy, broken. My clothes have dried to a crispy stiffness, and I can smell my own filth. I know I'm dirty as a pig in a sty, but I close my eyes to the world and wish I didn't ever have to wake up.

I dream about seeing Josy, Daddy, and Mama. They're all on a freight train with me, but we're ridin' on the top, not inside. They're angry at me for somethin', and we're arguing. Daddy looks so mad, madder than I've ever seen him. Mama looks disappointed in me, shaking her head in pity. Josy looks like he's about to disown me as a sister. But I cain't figure out what I did wrong. They won't tell me.

I feel so heavy in my heart, so downtrodden, and so frustrated that I cain't fix whatever's wrong. They start chargin' toward me, and I back up, lookin' over my shoulder, and they're pushin' me to the end of the train car, and I scream and shout, but they keep comin', and Josy reaches out and shoves me, and I fly over the end of the train and tumble down to the tracks, and right before I die, I look up and they're laughing at me.

I jolt awake, breathin' heavy. It's morning. People are moving about the camp, and I can smell somethin' cookin'. I turn toward the kitchen building, and a group of people are sittin' around the firepit, eatin' and chattin'. And there's Mary and her kids.

Before I gather the energy to get up, Mary starts walkin' toward me, kids in tow. She sits on an upturned bucket and eyes me. She looks concerned.

"I heard about what happened to you on the train," she says softly.

"What?" I'm shocked and scared. Barney may have been a bad man, but he likely has family. What if someone ain't happy about what I done?

"You ain't in trouble," Mary assures me. "They all said he attacked you, tried to steal your gun, and you was just defendin' yourself."

"Yeah, but—"

"But nothin'. You did what you had to do."

I cain't do nothin' but whimper.

"I'd have done the same thing. Anybody come after me or my little'uns? I'd kill 'em. But I'd do it on purpose, not on accident. You gotta watch yourself out here."

I nod, but I cain't say that I feel any better.

"Come on and get yourself somethin' to eat. Henry made scrambled quail eggs, and we fried up some ham. There's cracklings." She raises her eyebrows, 'cause cain't nobody say no to cracklings, and she knows it.

I clamber outa the sleepin' bag and get myself up to my feet. A dizzy spell makes me stop and reach out for somethin' to hold onto, but all that's there is Mary. When I grab her arm,

I feel nothin' but lean muscle, and I wonder how long she's been on the rails, raisin' her boys by herself. I wonder what she's had to see and what she's had to do. If she's ever killed a man.

"I was attacked once," she says as we eat our ham and eggs. We picked a spot in the woods, away from the others, to sit and eat and talk. "Only once. I did what I had to do to protect myself."

Her eyes slide toward her gun.

"What did you do?"

"Cain't you guess? I tell you what, ain't nobody messed with me since."

"So you...?" I feel sad for Mary. And scared.

I stand quickly and I'm shakin' and panickin'. *I cain't live this life. I cain't go around killin' people and sittin' and eatin' breakfast with people who go around killin' people.* I start pacin', and I'm drowning out all the sounds around me, and I'm so, so scared.

Mary takes my hand and leads me back to where I was sittin'. "You're okay," she says, but there's no conviction in her voice. She knows what I'm thinkin' and what I'm feelin'.

"Look, we're women. That makes us a target," she says, and then she pushes up her coat sleeve as far as it will go, and she makes a muscle and says, "We have to be strong. If I didn't have my gun, who knows what that man woulda done? Now nobody can touch me. And lord knows Barney sure as hell won't either, wherever he is. Prison, probably."

I freeze. Surely it's not. It cain't be. "D-did you s-say Barney?"

"Barney was my monster of a husband until I left him a year ago. Haven't seen him since."

I'm still frozen, my mouth hanging open. What if it was the same Barney? What if I killed Mary's husband?

She must notice my petrified face, 'cause she says, "What's the matter?"

Not knowing whether I'm makin' a mistake or not, I answer, "The man I—" I gulp. "The man who fell off the train... they said his name was Barney."

I cain't tell what Mary's reaction is, if it's good or bad. "Did he have dark bushy hair and beady black eyes?"

"I think so... yes. Skinny, too. And he was drunk."

Mary's eyes grow slim, and a grin appears on her face as she rocks back on her stool. "Well, I'll be." And she's noddin' like she's proud of me.

She leans forward, closer to me, looks straight into my eyes and says, "I wish I coulda been there to see it."

24

A Prayin' Girl

After gettin' back on the rails, I'm grateful that Dan and Glenn dried my blanket and extra clothes by the fire while I slept. My bag is mostly dry. Henry gave me some food to bring along. "Not all hobos are bad people, young'un," he'd said. "Matter fact, most of 'em are good folks, like Dan and Glenn over there."

I've come to believe that's true, considering how much help I've had on this journey. I don't think I coulda survived if it wasn't for the good folks I've met along the way. Rump, Mama Helen, Mary, Henry, and Dan and Glenn. Thinkin' about their kindness helps take my mind offa what I done. I killed a man. And even if he was an evil man, I committed the greatest sin. That does somethin' to a girl.

Now when my fingers find the gun in my pack, it almost stings, and I yank my hand back. I gotta think of another way to get even with Paul. He has to pay, but not with his life.

Dan scoots over and nudges me with his elbow. "Looks like you got some serious thoughts on your mind."

Dan looks to be about forty years old and has kind eyes, a

soft brown that reminds me of autumn leaves. He don't look scary like some of these other hobos who are so covered in dirt and grime that I think they musta been hobos all their lives. No, Dan looks clean-cut, like somehow he takes a bath every day and cuts his hair and trims his beard and cleans out his fingernails. I half expect to learn he has an office job in a city somewhere and just rides freight trains for entertainment.

Maybe he could help me figure out what to do. It's hard not havin' Josy to talk things through with, and Mama. Of course, I know what Mama'd say.

"Well," I start, not sure how much to tell, "a couple years ago, my older brother was ridin' the rails, findin' work and bringin' money back home to help pay the mortgage on the farm."

Dan nods like he understands completely. For all I know, he's done the same thing. Maybe he has a family waitin' for him somewhere.

"Then some mean ol' bulls caught him." This part is harder to tell than I thought it would be. "They beat him up real bad. His friends brought him home, but ... he didn't survive."

"Shoot," Dan whispers, shaking his head.

"Later, I went train-hoppin' – my mama and daddy needed help, and it was all I could do. I found work on a farm, thanks to this man named Paul Burnett. And, well, I thought I was fallin' for him, too." I watch Dan's eyes, and there's no ridicule in them, so I continue. "Anyway, when I went home, I found out my daddy had hung himself..."

Dan puts a gentle hand on my arm. "That kinda thing's been happenin' a lot these days, but I'm sorry it happened to your family."

"He was so depressed, and after that, my mama never was

the same again. And, well, she died earlier this month."

A tear trails down my cheek, and I look at Dan, who's wipin' his face as well.

"Here's what I need help with. Paul Burnett? The one I fell for? I found out that he was the railroad bull that beat up my brother."

I pause to let that sink in, and Dan's eyes are wide and he looks stunned.

"So he killed my brother, and I believe he's the reason both my parents are dead, too."

Dan lowers his head for a long while, his arms restin' on his knees. "You said you need help. Did talkin' about it help?"

"I don't mean that kinda help. I, uh, I planned to kill him. Brought my gun and—"

I stop talkin' when I see Dan's reaction. He looks like he's liable to jump off this train right here and now just to get away from me.

"Don't worry!" I hold up my hands. "I realized I cain't do that. After what happened… I know I cain't take a man's life. No matter what he done."

Relief washes over Dan's entire body, and he relaxes against the wall of the train car. "In that case, my dear, how can I help you?"

I shrug, because I honestly don't know. Maybe I did just need to talk about it. Say it out loud. And maybe now I can go home. "Well, I still feel like he cain't just get away with it. Like, I gotta make him pay somehow."

"Ahh," Dan says, "good ol' revenge." He turns and sits Indian style, facin' me. "I know the feeling of wanting revenge so badly. And you think it's gonna make you feel better. But here's what I've learned over the years: No revenge tastes as sweet as forgiveness."

I wrinkle up my eyebrows. "What do you mean, that I should just forgive him?"

He senses my anger rising and puts his hands on my shoulders. "I know it sounds crazy, but take it from me. You're only gonna feel better and get rid of the nasty feelings for good if you can forgive. You think I coulda lived this long and stayed this handsome by following vengeful ideas?"

He grins and winks, makin' me laugh. I lean back against the wall and think about what he said. How can I just forgive Paul? He flat-out ruined my life, and now I have nothing.

"You a prayin' girl?" Dan asks.

I don't know how to answer, 'cause I certainly used to be. But now I ain't so sure.

"There's your answer, young'un. God can help you much better than I can."

So I close my eyes and pray and pray and pray.

25

Cancer

When I make the final jump of my journey, everything looks so familiar, right down to the red maples that line the railroad. The ditch that I slipped and slid down when I was new to jumpin'. The low-hanging clouds that dust the treetops. The railyard building, where I first met Paul.

It's mid-afternoon, and the parking lot is full. I'm surprised I didn't see any bulls around, or at least railyard workers. Is this Sunday? Then I laugh, 'cause I honest-to-God have no idea what day it is. No one saw me jump. I decide to try my luck. I walk toward the building and pull open the door.

There's a man at an information desk, behind a window with a little hole in it. "May I help you?" he asks without looking up from his paperwork.

I clear my throat. "Um. I'm looking for Paul Burnett."

Now he looks up, and he flinches quite noticeably. He stares at me for some time before answering. "Mr. Burnett no longer works here. Hasn't in over a year."

Shocked, all I can manage to say is, "Oh." I want to ask

where he works now or what happened to him, but the man behind the window is looking at me like he really wants me to leave. It dawns on me that I haven't cleaned myself, or even brushed my hair or teeth, in I-don't-know-how-long, and I must look a complete mess.

"Anything else?" he asks.

"Um. Yes, please, is there a ladies' room I could use?"

He starts to shake his head, but I cain't let this chance go. "I'll be quick, I promise."

Thank the Lord, he points me in the direction of the restroom, and at last I get a chance to use a real toilet. Then, when I get a look at myself in the mirror, I can understand the man's hesitation. I need a bit more than to powder my nose. But I promised I'd be quick, so I peel off my filthy clothes, dig some soap outa my pack, and get to work on the world's quickest standing-in-the-middle-of-a-restroom-with-cold-tap-water-in-December bath. I don't have a comb, so I run wet fingers through my hair, trying to get the tangles out. It's no use, so I tie my hair up in a knot and hope that it looks better than before. At least I'm able to get my face and hands clean.

Then I shove on my change of clothes, wrinkled and still slightly damp, but just a mite cleaner. They'll do. I dig for the toothbrush Margaret Ann put in my pack – my goodness, was that only a few days ago? There's no toothpaste, so I use some water and scrub, scrub, scrub.

With one last look at my gaunt but now clean face, I put my coat back on and leave the restroom. "Thank you, sir. Oh, one more thing. What day is it?"

He looks mighty concerned when he answers, "It's Thursday the twenty-seventh."

I wave and high-tail it outa there, glad to finally know the date, but *crumbs, I shoulda asked for the time, too!* Well, that'd probably make the poor man more suspicious of me, as if he wasn't already suspicious enough.

So Paul don't work for the railroad anymore. I think on that as I walk toward the road that leads to the lane that turns into the drive that will take me to the Burnett farm. I wonder if he was fired. Maybe he beat up one too many hobos. Now my mind goes into the endless loop of being angry and wanting to take revenge and then back to thinking maybe I should forgive him like Dan said. My hatred of Paul is like a cancer I cain't get rid of no matter what. Praying didn't help me none, didn't give me any answers, as far as I can tell.

I wish Dan were here to help me through this. The last time I made this walk, I was with Pate, walkin' in the dark and in the rain. That was just before I learned the truth about Paul. What a horrible, horrible time that was. I don't even want to revisit how devastated I was, so instead, I focus on the beauty of Lafayette, Virginia.

Today is the most gorgeous December day I ever did see. The sun is low in the sky, and so are the clouds. It's chilly and crisp, but not too miserably cold. The mountains are topped with snow like a dollop of whipping cream on pecan pie. I can hear snow geese in a nearby lake, and winter birds are warbling in the trees. The soft wind carries the woodsy fragrance of chimneys and smoke houses.

When I start smelling home cookin', I know I'm close, and I'm reminded of how much at home I felt here. Until I didn't. And here come the conflicting feelings again, like my heart is in a wrestling match with itself.

And before I know it, here I am, on the drive that leads up to the Burnett farm, and all these emotions nearly knock me to my knees. The picture-perfect farm and house and barn all look the same, except now they're brushed with the muted colors of winter. How I loved it here. The scenery, the animals, the family. I remember the feeling of wanting to go home and not wanting to leave all at the same time. Being back here feels surreal, especially since I wasn't invited.

I realize now that I shoulda taken some time to really think of a plan. I mean, what am I gonna do now that I've decided I cain't kill Paul? What am I here for? I think about what Dan told me about forgiveness allowing a person to move forward and not have bad feelings anymore. I guess that's what I want — closure. I need the cancer gone. And to get that, according to Dan, I need to forgive Paul. So I guess I'm here to tell him I forgive him? But I hate him. Maybe I should tell him that I hate him but forgive him anyway.

As I'm lost in my thoughts, I realize two things. First thing is that I'm standin' here in the middle of the Burnett family's drive out in the open for all to see. And the second thing is that Paul's sister Laura just came out onto the porch with her baby, and she sees me, and I see her see me.

"June? Is that you?"

I consider turning around and runnin', but that would be silly, since someone's already seen me. Besides, I'm thrilled to see that Laura had her baby, 'cause I was worried about her being sick and all when I was here last year. I close the distance between us quickly.

"Hi! Yes, it's me." I smile real big, and it's a real smile — not one of those fake ones you make so's people think you're happy to see them. I really am happy to see her. "Your baby!"

Laura's smilin' too. "Yeah, this is Little Jerry, goin' on ten months old."

And we're standin' there smilin' like loons until she finally says, "Girl, come on up here and gimme a hug!"

We hug, with the baby squeezed between us, and he

giggles up a storm, which sends us to laughin', and that's when Laura says sadly, "Boy, that's the first time I've laughed in a looong time."

"Why? What's wrong?" I ask, my smile turnin' to a frown.

Her eyes turn dark and serious. "Oh," she says, hesitating. "Well, Mama's real sick. She's got the cancer."

26

I Still Hate Him

Louise Burnett is laid up in her bed, where she stays now all the time, and when I see her, I cain't keep the tears from flowin'.

"Well, Lord almighty, look what the cat drug in!" She sounds better than she looks, propped up on pillows against her headboard. On the other side of her bed is a toilet chair, like an old-fashioned chamber pot. On the nightstand are several medication bottles and a glass of water. She waves her hand, beckoning me over to her. I approach her bed slowly, but she grabs my hand and pulls me into a bear hug.

"June Baker, sweet girl, you look all grown up." She releases me, and before I can respond, she turns her head and coughs heavily into a bucket. "Ugh, this cough. No worries, though. How you been, and what are you doin' here?"

She pats the bed, indicating for me to sit down. "Well, uh…" I hadn't thought about this part, hadn't planned on actually talkin' to anyone, since all I was gonna do was kill Paul and leave (which sounds asinine now that I think about it).

"Um. My mama died, and—" Just sayin' those words to Mrs. Burnett makes my face crumple and a sob boil up.

She pulls me to her again and pats my back. "You poor thing. I'm so, so sorry."

She don't ask me to tell no more, and I'm glad of that 'cause I don't know if I could. So she does the talkin' now.

"The Lord works in mysterious ways, now, don't he? I'm sick with the cancer, I'm sure Laura told you. I can't hardly get outa bed no more. Doctor says I don't have much time left. A few months, maybe."

I'm speechless. A few *months*? She's about to die, and here she is soundin' cheerful. What could she possibly be cheerful about? I wonder then if me and mama woulda been cheerful if we had known a few months ago that she was gonna die. What would we have done with her last few months?

"I think he brought you to me just at the right time," Mrs. Burnett says. "You can help around here and cheer me up with your company."

I nod and nod and nod. Of course I will help. Mrs. Burnett was like a second mama to me, and I will do whatever needs doin'. She holds my hands in hers, and she starts talkin' to Laura about settin' up my old room, and in walks Paul.

I wasn't prepared for this, didn't expect him to just walk right on in, so by instinct, I smile at him, then realize I'm smilin' at the man I hate and until a day ago wanted to kill, so I real quick wipe the smile off my face. He stops short in the doorway, and he's standin' there starin' at me like I got two heads or somethin'.

"June," he says, his voice just above a whisper.

"Laura, why don't you and the baby come sit and keep me company while Paul and June talk in the living room?" Mrs. Burnett says.

Laura nods. "Sadie's makin' supper. It'll be ready shortly," she tells us, and she scoots around to the chair on the other side of the bed.

Paul's still starin' at me, and I'm tryin' not to look at him. "Y'all go on to the living room," Mrs. Burnett says. "I'll be alright. I'm sure you got some catchin' up to do."

But I don't know if I'm ready to be in the same room as him. Alone. What am I gonna say? Paul turns and leaves, and Mrs. Burnett nudges me off the bed, so I follow.

In the living room, we both stand silently, neither of us wanting to be the first one to talk, and we listen to the sounds of cookin' comin' from the kitchen. Finally, Paul says, "It's good to see you again."

I try not to look at his hazel eyes, his perfectly rugged dirty-blond hair, his broad shoulders and muscular arms. I'm reminded of the first time we met, when I looked a mess from train hoppin', and here he was, lookin' like a movie star. I imagine I must look even worse now, even though I cleaned up at the rail yard.

"You train hoppin' again?" He asks, a worried expression on his face.

I'm not sure what to say. "Um... I guess." I don't want to tell him about Mama. I don't feel like I owe him any explanation at all. If anyone owes someone something, it's him. He owes me an explanation and an apology. Big time.

My anger starts to build again, and I have to say something, but I don't know how to start, what to say, how to get my intentions across, so I blurt out, "It's all your fault, Paul!" And my anger turns to tears, which makes me even more furious 'cause I'm so tired of cryin' that I could just kill somebody. And that thought makes me laugh, so now I really look like a crazy person 'cause one minute I was shoutin', then

I was cryin', and now I'm laughin', and I don't even know what in the world to do with myself.

Paul steps forward, then backs away, then hesitates, and I can see his confusion about what to do, and I certainly understand it, yes sir. So he stays where he is and reaches out a hand, even though he's too far away to actually reach me, which I'm glad of, 'cause I don't want him to touch me.

"June, we need to talk," he says gently. "I have so much to explain, and so many questions to ask, too."

I cain't imagine what in the world he has to ask me, but we don't get a chance to say nothin' else, 'cause Mr. Burnett and Laura's husband, Gregory, come in, with Granny and Pawpaw trailin' behind and yappin' up a storm.

When they see me, they erupt in cheers and hellos and then we're all huggin' and makin' small talk, and I hardly notice when Paul slips out of the room and sneaks down the hall.

I try to make sense of what I'm feeling, but I'm so exhausted that I push it outa my mind. Try to enjoy a delicious homecooked meatloaf and green beans and iced tea kissed by lemon, and a blackberry cobbler for dessert. I eat so much I'm fit to burst at the seams.

I hardly even notice that Paul ain't at the table durin' dinner, but Laura says, "Paul eats with Mama every night, feeds her the best he can."

So now I'm tryin' to hate him while he's feedin' his dyin' mama instead of eatin' at the table with the rest of the family.

But I still do. I still hate him.

27

Arrested

The work begins immediately, with dishes to be washed, bedding to be changed, floors to be swept, medicine to be given, and so much more that they don't make me do. And it's now, as the nighttime approaches, that I realize they have electricity at the farm now. They have two lamps in the living room, and one in all the other rooms. Even the tiny space they named "June's Room," which used to be the maid's quarters, upstairs next to the second-floor porch.

That porch was one of my favorite spots when I was here last year. I go out there now, and am startled to find Paul standin' there. He holds up his hands, palms facing me, like a surrender.

"I just wanted to say that we can talk tomorrow," he says, eyebrows raised. "If that's okay. I mean, if you want. I'd really like to talk to you. Tomorrow. Tomorrow." And he backs out the door and disappears.

I turn to the majestic view and lean on the porch railing.

It's dark now, but the moon is big and bright and bathes the rolling hills in silver and purple. *Tomorrow.* I have until tomorrow to come up with what to say to Paul.

Laura shows me to the new washroom, with a toilet and a shower, inside the house, and it feels so good to get clean. It's the cleanest I've been since I stayed at Margaret Ann's house. And then I sleep the most glorious sleep in the history of sleeps, and I ain't even exaggeratin'. I don't toss or turn or dream or squirm one bit. And I wake up refreshed and ready to take on whatever the day may bring.

And bring things it does, 'cause right away, I'm helpin' with cleanin' up after breakfast (I slept through the eatin' part), and then I'm helpin' Laura with gettin' Mrs. Burnett up to walk a bit, stretch her legs. That leads to cleanin' up vomit and spilt water. And then I'm playin' with Little Jerry so that Laura can do the clothes washin'. Sadie's out in the barn tendin' to the animals, and I don't know where all the men went. Granny and Pawpaw are sittin' with Mrs. Burnett while she rests.

It ain't long before Paul comes in, wipin' his boots on the doormat, and when Little Jerry spots him, he squeals with delight and holds his arms up. Paul swoops down and picks him up and tosses him gently into the air and catches him, and it's all laughter and giggles.

"Oooooh, Little Jerry-Jerry loves Uncle Paul-Paul," Paul coos while the baby grabs at his face and laughs. They play like that for a minute, until the baby starts fussin', and Paul says it's time for his nap. Paul fetches a small bottle from the kitchen and fills it with a little milk and some powder formula. He screws the top on and presses the nipple down with his forefinger so that it won't leak when he shakes it up to mix it.

I stand and watch as he expertly completes this routine, and Little Jerry pants and begs at Paul's legs. Then he scoops the little one up and cradles him in his arms, and the baby grabs the bottle and goes to town drinkin'. Before he heads down the hall, Paul looks back at me and says, "Meet you on our porch in five minutes?"

I nod. *Our porch.* Funny, I always thought of it as our porch, too. I shake my head to try to force away these feelings. I still hate him.

I'm not waitin' on the porch long. He practically skips through the door, apologizin' for takin' so long.

Once we're sittin' down, awkwardly lookin' at each other while at the same time tryin' not to look at each other, Paul says, "So, June, tell me why you're here. I have a suspicion you're not here looking for work."

I decide to be honest, 'cause I'm pretty tired of hemmin' and hawin'. "I came to kill you."

Paul flinches and his eyes go wide, and his hands are on the arms of the porch chair like he's gonna get up, but he stays put. "O-okay. Now, tell me why?"

And I'm mad again. "*Why?* Are you crazy? Did you forget? I came here to kill you because you killed my brother! And because of that, my daddy killed himself! And because of that, my mama died of a broken heart! And I don't think you oughta be able to get away with all of that!"

He holds his hands up, and he looks stunned. "Whoa, whoa, let's just— let's calm down and talk about this. I think there's been a misunderstanding."

"What are you talkin' about?"

"Well, I … I didn't kill your brother."

"What? Yes you did! You were the mean ol' railroad bull who beat him up."

"No! I mean, yes, I was there, and I was— I saw it. But I wasn't the one who beat him up."

Confusion and numbness spread through my body. How can this be? "What do you mean?"

"I was workin' with another guy that day, a guy named Jeff. Now, Jeff's a real hothead, and I hated workin' with him. But anyways, when we found these three guys on a freighter, one of 'em was mouthin' off. Jeff decided he wanted to rough 'em up. He went for the colored kid first, but your brother—your brother went after Jeff. So Jeff threw the colored kid to me and told me to hold him, and he started punchin' your brother."

My eyebrows wrinkle up as I try to make sense of this new story. "So you're tellin' me that Pate was lyin' that night when he saw you in your kitchen and told me you were the one who beat up Josy?"

"No, I don't think he was lying," Paul says. "I think he just made a mistake.

"I don't believe he was wrong about that. Do you remember the fear on his face? I do, 'cause it's etched into my brain."

"I know, I know, but June, you'd understand if you saw Jeff."

I cross my arms and shake my head. I don't know what to believe, but this sounds crazy.

Paul stands up and holds his hand out. "Come on. Come with me. It'll only take a few minutes."

I push myself up from the chair without takin' his hand and follow him reluctantly down the stairs and outside to a truck.

"I don't know what you're tryin' to do here or what this is supposed to prove," I say, stompin' my feet.

"Just get in," Paul says. "I promise what I'm gonna show you is important."

The tires kick up dust as he swerves outa the drive and onto the lane. I keep my arms crossed and a scowl on my face the whole time, but when he stops the truck in front of a library, my arms come undone and my face softens, almost smiles. *A library.* I ain't been to a library in so long, I hadn't realized how much I missed it 'til now.

We get outa the truck and I follow him through the door and to the circulation desk, where he asks the librarian to see a newspaper from February eighteenth, nineteen thirty-four. I got no idea what the significance of that date is, and anyhow, I'm just standin' there lookin' around at all the books and wishin' I could browse and check out a whole armful.

When the librarian returns with a newspaper, Paul leads me to a table, where he sets the paper down and flips the pages until he finds what he's lookin' for.

"There," he says, pointin' to a small story in the paper with a tiny picture.

I bend down closer and read the headline. *Railroad policeman arrested for freighter beatings.*

"What's this?" I ask Paul. "Who is this?"

"Look at the picture," he insists.

When I look, I almost jump backward. The man in the photo looks just like Paul, a remarkable resemblance. The only difference I can see is the nose is a little more crooked, and it's hard to tell from the little black-and-white photo, but the hair might be darker.

"Now look at the name and read the story," Paul says.

I read aloud.

> *Jeffrey Donahue, 20, an employee of Virginia Railways, was arrested yesterday on multiple charges,*

including the beatings of two vagrants in the Salem area,
between Lafayette and Roanoke. One of the vagrants
was identified as Charlie Walsh of Kentucky. The other
was unidentified but was said to have come from
Tennessee. A railroad spokesperson, who spoke on
condition of anonymity, said the investigation is being
handled and that the employee has been terminated.

There's more, but I stop there and look up at Paul. "Josy? It's talkin' about Josy? The unidentified Tennessee man?"

"Yes, it is." Paul nods, looking at me, waiting for my reaction.

And Charlie! He beat up Charlie too? I remember Pate sayin' he never saw Charlie again but that he thought he got away from the bulls. I'm stumped. Stunned.

"But Josy died in March of ninety-three. This man wasn't arrested until this year," I say, confusion in my eyes.

"Jeff— he was a wildcard. He beat people up everywhere we went, but no one was brave enough to tell on him. After what happened with your brother, and findin' out that he kept beatin' on him at the jail, even though those friends of his came to try to get him out, well, I'd seen enough. I went to the boss. He told me he'd look into it, but I know he didn't. I kept hearin' more stories about Jeff punchin' people around. And then I met you, and you told me about your brother dyin' and all. So I went to the boss again. This time he got angry with me, so I didn't push it. I wish I would have."

Paul looks down, regret heavy on his shoulders. I'm paralyzed, rooted to my spot next to him.

"After you left me your marble and went home, I just had to do something. So I went back to the boss and insisted he do something about Jeff. He not-so-kindly showed me the door."

I gasp. "You mean you got fired?"

"Yep." Paul shrugs his shoulders like it ain't a big deal. "The thing is, other people started rattin' Jeff out too. See, everyone knows that railroad bulls rough up the tramps every now and then, but Jeff always took it too far. He was bad news, and that's bad for the railroad company. So finally they decided to take care of it, and they went diggin' and found witnesses. I testified and everything."

"You did?" My heart leaps with gratitude. And a little bit of jealousy that I didn't get to testify against that mean ol' bull myself. "But, Paul, why didn't you tell me all this? You left me that letter and you didn't tell me none of this."

Paul sighs and sits down. I sit down with him. "June, I— I felt so guilty that I didn't stop Jeff that day. I stood there holdin' onto the colored kid—"

"Pate," I interrupt.

"Pate," Paul says. "Sorry. I stood there and watched. I couldn't believe my eyes when Jeff kept goin', kept punchin' and kickin'. I hollered at him, but I— I shoulda done more."

He puts his head in his hands and groans.

"Why didn't you?" I ask, softly, curiously. "Do more?"

Without lookin' at me, he whispers, "I guess I was afraid. Didn't know what to do. Jeff was tougher than me. Scarier."

I take it all in, remembering our conversations on the farm last year.

"That time you came into the barn with your hand all bruised up?"

He smirks. "I punched a wall. That was after the second time the boss blew me off."

"Then why'd you tell me you punched a train-hopper?"

"I don't know. I guess that sounded more exciting than 'I

was throwing a fit and hit a wall.'"

We sit there for a long time not sayin' anything before Paul sniffles and sits up. "We, uh … better get back. I gotta get the truck back home."

We're still quiet almost all the way back, but before we turn into the Burnett farm, Paul asks, "Can you forgive me?"

I cain't answer right away. I just cain't. "Can you give me some time to think about all this?"

He nods. "Of course."

I head back into the house and Paul heads out to the barn, and now my brain is spinning with so much information that I feel dizzy and sick to my stomach. So I go up to sit with Mrs. Burnett. If anyone can make me feel better right now, it's her.

28

Bullets

When I enter Mrs. Burnett's room, she's squirming around in her bed, the lunch tray on her lap tilting and threatening to flip over and spill her lunch everywhere.

"Mrs. Burnett! What's wrong?"

"What's *not* wrong, sweet thing? And how many times have I told you to call me Louise?"

I hold my arms out, like I'm gonna steady her, but I got no idea what she's tryin' to do or what she's on about.

"I need to get to my pot," she groans.

My pot ... my po— oh! "Uh ... okay, let me get your lunch up off you 'fore it spills."

I grab the tray, a full bowl of soup sloshing as I lift it.

"You hardly touched your lunch, Mrs. Burnett." And that reminds me that I haven't eaten lunch either, but for some reason I just ain't hungry.

As I turn to set the tray on the bedside table, I lose my balance and slam the tray down a little too hard, sending three bottles of pills and the bowl of soup crashing to the floor.

"Oh no!"

"Ugh," Mrs. Burnett moans. "Don't worry about that now. Come over here and help me."

I rush to the other side of the bed and grab her hands, forgetting for a moment that mine are covered in greasy broth. Mrs. Burnett pulls her hands back and grimaces.

"So sorry, Mrs. Burnett!" I wipe my hands on my pants while she uses a towel on hers.

"You best hurry, or there'll be a smelly mess in the bed to deal with," she warns.

"Oh! Okay, here." I take her hands again and step back to give her room to stand, but I back right into the toilet chair, knockin' it off-kilter.

"Lord almighty, June, you're in worse shape than I am!" she says as she grunts and lifts up off the bed. She says it funny, but her face is a snarl. I'm starin', not sure what to do.

"You gotta hold me steady so I can get these underpants down and sit."

So I hold as steady as I can while she leans on me with her right arm and tries to undress with her left arm. Finally, she starts to lower herself onto the toilet, but her weight pulls me down on top of her, and I'm not even exaggeratin', I land splat on the pot with her, my face right in her bosom, and I ain't never been so embarrassed in my whole entire life.

Mrs. Burnett is hollerin' and I'm hollerin', and then Sadie comes into the room. Sadie, who never really took to me, who thought I was trouble. Her eyes look at us in horror, then flick to the wasted soup and the spilled pills beside the bed.

"What in the world?" She races to us as I struggle back to my feet, my face red as a lobster, Mrs. Burnett's white as a sheet.

"Mama, are you okay?" Sadie whines, shooting me a scowl as I scamper out of the room.

And there it is: proof that I could never become a nurse or a caretaker or even a mama as long as I live. I run out to the mule barn and find the Burnetts' three mules huddled up in their stalls, blankets on, as the weather seems to have taken a chilly turn. This is where I belong – with animals rather than people.

I visit with the mules I once called F, D, and R, until I learned their real names, which I've forgotten now. These mules are so lovable, they make me miss my Molly. Which makes me think about home. Mama. Jimmy. Would Jimmy be glad to know I didn't kill Paul? What he said about Josy still stings, so I put Jimmy outa my mind the best I can.

I spend the next few hours tryin' to hide out and steer clear of Sadie, who most certainly thinks I'm an incompetent fool after what she walked in on. And I feel terrible for not bein' a better helper for Mrs. Burnett. I know I just caused more work for everybody else, and they don't need that right now, what with all they got on their plates.

Later, I'm helpin' Laura with the baby, and Paul peeks in from the hallway. "Mama wants to see you, June."

He smiles, so I guess it cain't be that bad, but I'm shakin' like mad as I walk down the hall and peer around the corner into Mrs. Burnett's room.

"You get on in here, sweet thing," she hollers.

I step lightly and slowly toward her, and she pats the bed for me to sit down, and she looks into my eyes.

"I'm sorry I made you help me with that nasty chore. I shouldn't have."

"No, Mrs. Burnett, I'm the one that's sorry!"

"June, I have never known you to be clumsy," she says, all serious-like. "So what's gotten into you?"

I figure I'd better be honest, since she don't have much time left in this world, so I go ahead and unload it all. I tell her about what I thought Paul did, and what he really did. About what I came here to do, and what I really should do. About how I'm confused now and don't know what to do.

I'm scared to look up at her after telling her that I had plans to murder her only son, but she don't scold me or nothin', just pulls me into her arms.

"You have had so much tragedy in your life, and I understand needin' to have somebody to blame for it all. But I also know, now more than ever, that life is too short to waste time on anger, and what you really need, instead of someone to blame … is someone to love."

I sit up and look at her, and I think how wise she is.

"My Paul has made mistakes," she says, shakin' her head. "Takin' that railroad police job was a big one, and he knew it. But when you came to us last year, you brought a light to this whole family, Paul included. I think he would do anything for you, and I also think you two have the makings of a wonderful friendship. You are always welcome in this family."

"Thank you, Mrs. Burnett."

"Uh-uh!" She gives me a warning look.

"Louise. Thank you, Louise."

"Now, go see about helpin' with supper."

"Okay. I'll come back later to help you with whatever you need."

Her face fills with worry, and she says, "Oh, no, you don't need to help me none. Just come to tell me goodnight."

She laughs and I laugh and she lays her head down and I head up to my room. And walk right into Paul. He's standin' in the middle of my room, holdin' my gun.

I march in there and shout, "What are you doing in here?" Not angry, really, but surprised.

"This the gun you were gonna kill me with?" He spins it and tosses it up and catches it.

I hold up a hand in warning. "It's loaded!"

He empties it of its bullets, shakes them in his hand. "Could you have really done it, June? Put a bullet in me?"

I don't have an answer.

"What were you gonna aim for? Head? Heart?"

My shoulders sag, and I sit down hard on the bed.

"Where were you gonna do it? In front of Mama? In front of Laura and the baby? Granny and Pawpaw?"

My tears come fast. "That ain't fair, Paul."

"I know," he says, settin' the gun down beside me and pocketing the bullets. "None of this is fair." And he walks out.

29

At Home Again

After washin' up, I go down to the kitchen to see if I can help get supper ready. Sadie's choppin' celery and potatoes to put in a stew. Laura's flouring a pan for biscuits. I watch them work side by side for a minute before announcing my presence. The difference between the two is stark. Laura's hummin' softly as she works, swayin' side to side. Sadie is serious-faced, choppin' forcefully like she's takin' revenge on the cutting board.

I hear the baby cry from his room down the hall, and Laura turns. When she sees me, I say, "I'll go get him."

She flicks her eyes toward Sadie. "No, you take over in here for me. The biscuit dough just needs to be rolled out and cut." She wipes her hands on her apron, then takes it off and slips it over my head.

When I get to the counter and reach for the bowl of dough, an audible sigh comes from Sadie.

"That was crazy earlier, wasn't it? You walked in just at the worst time." I chuckle, like the memory of it was ages ago, somethin' we can all look back on and laugh about.

Sadie turns to throw celery ends in the trash bin. "Yep. Crazy." There's no lightness in her voice.

After a few minutes of silence, I decide to lay it all out in the open. "You don't feel too kindly for me, do you?"

She turns her head just a smidge and looks over her shrugging shoulder. "I don't feel one way or the other."

"Well, you don't treat me the way the others do."

Sadie puts her knife down and turns to face me fully. "I just like to get things done, and I like to get them done right. You're just a lovesick child. I think you oughta run along back home and play with your dolls, is all."

She turns around and continues choppin' and tossin' things in the stock pot while I stand there fuming. And I try so hard to bite my tongue, but I just cain't do it. I say as sweetly as I can, "Well, I'd rather be a lovesick child than a loveless old spinster."

I get to rollin' out the dough on parchment, and out of the corner of my eye, I see Sadie's mouth dropped open, practically catchin' flies, and I smile inside. I'm still shakin' with anger, though, so I take it out on the dough. These biscuits are liable to be flat as pancakes. I use an open tin can to cut circles in the dough, dust some flour onto them and plop 'em in the pan that Laura floured.

Laura comes back in time for me to whip the apron off and stride outa the room, beggin' the tears not to fall. She catches up with me and takes my arm.

"She's hard on you 'cause life's hard right now," Laura says. "It's nothin' to do with you."

I don't believe her, but I nod anyway and head out the back door to find somethin' to do outside, somewhere I ain't just a child in the way. I head to the chicken coop, then immediately wish I had stopped to get my coat.

"Well, you chickens are smarter than I am," I say as I kneel in the dirt by the coop's door. "Y'all got the sense to stay inside."

They cluck their greetings in soft warbles, a musical sound I've always loved. Two of 'em come up to the door to investigate, peck at my outstretched hand, but the rest of 'em stay put in their cozy nests.

"Naw, I ain't got nothin' for ya." I shiver in the wind and get to work cleanin' the chicken yard, the sun already hidden behind the mountains and darkness setting in. The mindless work of scoopin' chicken poop into a bucket to take to the compost bin gives me time to think about all that's been on my mind.

I understand that Paul wasn't to blame for Josy's death – at least not directly. But he was there, and he took part in it by holdin' Pate back. He watched. He didn't make it stop. That part I don't understand. Should I still hate him for the role he played, even though it was Jeffrey Donahue who did all the beating?

Of course, Paul did go to his boss about Jeff's violent side, multiple times, but was always shut down. Until he wasn't, and he eventually got Jeff arrested. Shouldn't that be grounds for forgiveness? Doesn't all that show that he's really a good person?

It makes my head hurt, all this thinkin'. I don't know how it's possible that I'm more confused than ever. When I first set out on this journey, I knew exactly what I wanted. Now, I know nothing.

I'm rakin' the ground to even out the chicken yard when the men come toward the house from the barns and the field, lookin' hot and sweaty even though it's thirty-somethin' degrees out. Paul pauses by the coop when he sees me.

"Gettin' dark," he says. "We're goin' in for supper. You comin'?"

I hook the rake in its notch on the side of the coop. "Yeah, I'm comin'."

The men head around to the back washroom, and I go in the front door and up to my room to wash up. The house smells deliciously of beef stew and biscuits, a welcome warmth after bein' outside with no coat.

At the dinner table, I avoid Sadie, and as usual, Paul makes a bowl for himself and a bowl for his mama and heads to her room. I watch as he goes, taken by what a sweet gesture that is. No, not just a gesture. It's a ritual, a bond between mother and son. And if I know Paul, it's his way of holding onto her a little bit longer, of making up for any wrongs he done.

When I snap out of my daze, I notice Sadie glare at me with her disapproving look, and I quickly step into the role of gettin' Little Jerry into his high chair and feedin' him while everyone else gets the table set for Mr. Burnett and Granny and Pawpaw and Laura's husband.

Little Jerry coos just like them silly chickens outside, and his smile brightens up the whole room, even enough to wipe the meanness off of Sadie's ol' face. So I try to focus on that. If nothin' else is right in the world, the sweetness of an innocent baby can bring light to the darkest spots and heaviest hearts.

And just like that, I feel at home again.

30

I Have a Place

On my third day at the Burnett farm, I write to Mr. and Mrs. Porter to let them know I'm safe. I tell them I'm staying with relatives, which ain't far from the truth. I also write to Margaret Ann. She needs to know that I didn't kill nobody and everything's alright.

I think about writin' Jimmy too, but after that fight we had, I figure he wouldn't want to hear from me. I slapped him. I cain't believe I *slapped* him. At the time, I was sure he deserved it. Now, I just feel embarrassed and regretful. But I'm no longer sure about my feelings for him. Bein' here again just brings back so much – it's like I'm in a different world, another life.

It don't take long for me to slip back into my routine here at the Burnett farm. Things are different since it's not harvest season, and since Mrs. Burnett is sick in bed, and since Paul ain't workin' for the railroad anymore, and since there's a baby in the house now. But other things are the same: everyone workin' together like a well-oiled machine, the happy chatter of Granny and Pawpaw, the wind tickling the wind chimes on the porch, the magnificent view from the upstairs balcony, the majestic hills that the cows and goats and horses explore.

It's easy to fall in love with this place, and this family fills the gaping hole in my heart that was ripped open little by little until it nearly swallowed me up. And it keeps me from dwelling on all that I've lost.

At first, I don't really have a set role here. I do whatever is needed of me – take care of the baby while Laura's cleanin' or cookin', wash and brush Mrs. Burnett's hair, clean the chicken coop, milk the cows, shovel snow, clean the rugs, run things to and from the cellar. And that seems to suit everyone just fine.

I stay out of Sadie's way and lean on the ones who love me. Even Mr. Burnett treats me like family. One night at supper, without any warning, he says, "June, why don't you say grace for us?"

Caught off guard, I think about the prayer they always said the last time I was here: *In a world where so many are hungry, may we eat this food with humble hearts.* I think for a moment about Mama, Daddy, Josy, Margaret Ann's daddy, and now Mrs. Burnett with her cancer. I clear my throat, we all clasp hands around the table, and I close my eyes.

"In a world where so many have lost so much, may we remember what we have with grateful hearts." I open my eyes to see pleased and impressed smiles, and there's a chorus of Amens before we dig in to our meal. Even Sadie glances at me without the hardness that usually rests on her face where I'm concerned.

Mr. Burnett, to my right at the head of the table, leans over and says, "Real nice prayer, June. Real nice."

I duck my head, cheeks rosy, but inside I'm pretty proud of myself. After supper, I offer to help clean the dishes, but Laura nudges me toward the hallway. "Sadie and I got the dishes. You go sit with Mama."

When I enter Mrs. Burnett's room, Paul's sittin' in the chair by her bed, and he stands when he sees me. He says, "Come on in," and Mrs. Burnett says, "There she is," at the same time, and I don't know why they seem so happy to see me.

I take my usual spot on the bed next to Mrs. Burnett, and she takes my shoulders in her hands, still strong and solid despite her illness. "June, what a wonderful prayer that was!"

I blink back my astonishment and look at Paul. "Y'all heard that?"

"We always listen to the supper prayer," he says.

"I really like what you did with our humble hearts prayer," Mrs. Burnett says. "I always knew you must be a writer."

"A writer?" I hadn't really thought about that. I guess I enjoyed writin' in school, especially when Miss Glass gave us somethin' fun to write about, and I do remember her tellin' me I had a gift for writin'. But I reckon the past three years or so I've had more important things on my mind than writin'.

"Or a poet," Paul says.

I snap my head to look at him, the significance of his statement not lost on me. He was the one who used to write little snippets of poetry and leave them in the pockets of my clothes hangin' on the line to dry. We hold each other's gaze until I'm uncomfortable enough to look away. I was hoping he'd be the first to look away.

"I do hope you'll do something with that talent, girl," Mrs. Burnett says. "I, for one, would love to read anything you write."

"Thank you, ma'am. Maybe I'll come up with some more prayers or somethin'."

"That would be very nice."

Paul leans over and hugs and kisses his mama, then says his goodbyes and takes his exit. When he's long past earshot, Mrs. Burnett sighs and asks, "Well, now, have you figured some things out since we last talked? You seem to be feeling better."

I think on that a spell. "I guess so. I mean, I'm still confused as ever about Paul, but you know what has made me feel better?"

"What's that?" I love how she leans back against her pillow, eyes glued to me like she's settling in for an important story.

"You," I say quietly, tryin' not to tear up. "You and your family. This house. This land. It's like ... everything I need."

Mrs. Burnett takes my hand in both of hers, patting gently. "Why, that's the absolute kindest and sweetest thing anybody has ever said, and it fills my heart, it really does. You're a good girl, June. Don't you forget that. And you can stay here as long as you need. As long as you want."

We sit in a cloud of admiration for a moment, and I leave the room knowing that I have a place, I have a family. And now what I told Mr. and Mrs. Porter really does feel like the truth.

31

Questions and Answers

I corner Paul in the mule barn the next morning. I don't know if it's the bravest thing to do or the stupidest, but I have questions that I desperately need answers for.

"Alright, good, 'cause I have a question for you, too," Paul says, "but you go first." He perches on the barn window, ankles crossed, hands in his coat pockets, lookin' like a young Buck Jones.

I take a deep breath, try to gather my thoughts, remember all the questions that have been spinning around in my head for the past three days, but I don't even know where to start. I pace the barn, rubbing my hands together.

"When you wrote me poems and little notes and left surprises in the laundry for me, last time I was here … why did you do those things?"

Paul chuckles. "What do you mean? I—"

"Well, when you—when I found them, I … I reckon I thought it meant something."

"I, uh, I guess I was just—"

"Okay, don't answer that. Let's just … move on." I don't think I want to hear his answer to that anyway, so I get to the more important stuff. "When the other railroad bull – Jeff – started beatin' on Josy, explain to me again why didn't you stop him."

Paul blows out a deep breath. "At first, it was just normal Jeff, you know? It's what we do when train-hoppers are givin' us trouble." He stands up off the window and starts his own pacing. "But … then he kept going, and I remember yelling at him to stop, but I was … I was scared."

He's lookin' down, his back toward me like he's ashamed, and I feel sorry for him. My brother was the one who died, and I'm standin' here feeling sorry for Paul. What kinda ridiculousness is that?

"Okay, so then you reported Jeff to your boss, again and again, you told me that. But how come you didn't come after me that night? The night I was there with Pate and he recognized you?"

He turns to look at me, and his eyes are watered up. "I thought you'd hate me. For bein' involved in…"

He lets his words trail off, and I think on that a spell. "But, Paul, because you didn't explain yourself right then and there, I went the next year thinkin' you were the one that killed Josy."

He steps toward me. "I know, I know that now, and I'm sorry." He holds his arms out like he may hug me but then turns away. "I'm so sorry."

We stand there, close but far apart at the same time. I think neither of us knows what to do or say. I want so badly to forgive him, and I think I do. And I think I know him better now. This big, bulky railroad bull – or former railroad bull – wasn't really cut out for bein' a railroad bull. He's like a sheep in wolf's clothing.

"Paul?" I decide to break the silence, and we meet each other's eyes. "What was it you wanted to ask me?"

Relief floods his face and he smiles. "Oh, right. Um, there's a New Year's Eve party. At that big hotel in Roanoke – you remember it?"

"Yes! The Lenox Hotel."

"That's the one." Paul looks nervous all of a sudden, fidgeting with the zipper of his coat, and I find it hilarious. Cute, even. "Tomorrow's New Year's Eve, and they're having a party there, at the Lenox."

"M'hm, you said that already." I'm really enjoying seeing him squirm.

He shakes his head, his face turnin' red. "Okay, so, would you go with me? To the party?"

"Sure, I guess. That'll be fine. Only—"

"Only what?"

"I don't have anything to wear to a fancy New Year's Eve party."

He reaches for my hand, and I let him take it. "Don't worry, June. Between Laura and Sadie and the clothes we still have of Claire's, I bet we can find you something suitable."

We walk together back toward the house, but I take my hand from his before we get there. I don't think I'm ready to hold his hand just yet. I need my initial question answered first.

32

New Year's Disaster

Dearest June,
I am so relieved that you didn't do it! I knew you couldn't. I think we both did. But, boy, is it good to hear that you didn't. When are you going home? I'll bet Jimmy misses you something awful. And don't you want to see Molly and Bug and all your Maynardville friends and neighbors? Well, you stay safe. When you do decide to go home, use the money I gave you for a train ticket, if you still have it.
Friends forever,
M.A.

My heart hurts to think that people are worried about me or missin' me, but the truth is, they probably haven't even noticed I'm gone. I live way out in the middle of nowhere, after all. I do miss Molly and Bug, and even the silly ol' chickens (JimBoJoe, especially). And I do miss Maynardville and church on Sundays. I miss our farm and our house. But that's the thing. *Our* is a thing of the past. There's no *our* anymore. It's just me. I'm all alone, and all alone, the house ain't gonna feel like home. And besides, I cain't stay there by myself until I'm a legal adult. If I'm lucky, I may be able to get away with stayin' home on my own at seventeen, if everybody keeps their mouths closed about it, that is. So the way I see it, I've got at least nine months before I can go back.

And Jimmy? Now both my heart and my head hurt. Aw, crumbs, he's probably moved on by now anyhow. What does he need with me?

I wonder what Margaret Ann would say if she knew I spent all her money on a gun to kill Paul with, and now I'm about to go to a New Year's Eve party with him. It's not a date or anything, we're just going. Together. Is it a date? Laura found me a dress to wear, fancier than I've ever worn before. It's blue with silver sequins and three-quarter sleeves. The neckline swoops down like a heart, the bodice is fitted, and the skirt falls smoothly to my ankles. The only shoes I have are work boots, so Laura lent me a pair of flats. My feet slip and slide in them, but it's better than wearing work boots.

I sit on a stool in the washroom while Laura braids my hair and twists it up in a beautiful "up do," as she calls it. She suggests a pair of earrings, but my ears aren't pierced.

"That's okay," she says. "These are clip-ons. Look." And she clips one onto each ear and lets me look in the mirror.

"Wow!" I cain't believe it. With my hair and makeup done, I don't even recognize the young woman staring back at me. A fancy young woman.

"I know!" Laura giggles. "You are stunning, young June."

I admire myself for a moment, wondering what Paul will think.

"Now for the last touch," Laura says, and she spritzes me

with some perfume.

When I step quietly down the stairs, Paul is standing there in the living room, and he's wearing a black suit with a white shirt and tie, and his hair's all slicked back. He's ... he's ... well, gorgeous is the first word that comes to mind. That's when he looks up and notices me, and my face is as red hot as a fire engine, 'cause now this really feels like a date.

"You're sparkling," he says, smilin' ear to ear.

I nod, too nervous to speak. Then he hands me a single red rose, and I'm relieved it's been de-thorned.

"Well, you ready to go?" he asks, and again, I nod.

As soon as we step outside, I regret wearin' this dress. It's freezin' cold! I try to tough it out, but by the time we get to Mr. Burnett's truck, I'm shiverin' and my teeth are practically chatterin' out loud. Paul takes his suit coat off and drapes it around my shoulders before opening the passenger door and helping me into the truck, and now I'm drenched in the scent of Paul, and my heart is warm.

After a ride of awkward silence, I'm amazed when we get to downtown Roanoke. The buildings are lit up in twinkling lights, there are laughing couples in dresses and suits, there's music comin' from somewhere, and cars everywhere.

The sun has sunken down behind hills, so the air is much colder than when we left the farm. As Paul circles a parking lot in search of a spot, I hug his coat tighter around myself and gaze out this window, then that one, then the back window, simply in awe of ... everything.

Just like the first time I came to the Burnett farm, I feel like I've stepped into another world, where there is no Depression and no grief. I hardly even think about how an hour ago there was probably a line of folks right here waitin' for food from the soup kitchen. And how tomorrow morning, all this cheer will be swept away to be replaced by another line of people in need.

I even forget about the cold wind as we step up to the corner windows of the Lenox Hotel, where folks are gathered and waiting to be let in. Everything looks different at night, and especially on this special night, the hotel is transformed into a glittery, glowing palace. When I see the maître-d' taking tickets and opening a velvet rope for one glamorous couple at a time, I wonder how in the world Paul could afford this.

As if he read my mind, Paul leans in and says in my ear, "I have an uncle who's friends with the owner." Then he shakes hands with the maître-d' and points to a line on a list of names the man has on a clipboard. And then he's ushering me into the hotel and into a ballroom, and suddenly I'm flushed with warmth.

I hand Paul his coat without taking my eyes off of the heavy, embroidered drapes, the grand piano, the shiny checkered floor, the enormous three-tiered chandelier hanging in the center of the room and sending sparkling light onto the tables surrounding the dance floor.

Guests are milling about and mingling, all diamonds and smiles. I feel so out of place. I'm not a fancy girl. I'm a farm girl in a costume. Paul senses my unease and guides me to an open table and pulls out a seat for me.

"June, are you okay?"

"Yes, I just—it's overwhelming."

Paul nods and asks if I want something to eat or drink, but I feel dizzy, like I might throw up if I move, or if I look around at the couples twirling and swirling around the dance floor, and the twinkling chandelier, and the rich, heavy drapes, and the checkered floor that now looks like it's moving, and the piano, whose keys are being pounded by someone madly and loudly playing a Duke Ellington song while someone else blows into a saxophone (or is it a trumpet?), the swirling couples, the twinkling lights, the moving floor, the pounding piano, the couples, the lights, the floor, the—

"Can we get some air?"

Paul takes my elbow and leads me out of the ballroom, grabbing a glass of water on the way, and we duck out a side door. The blast of chilly wind on my face makes me feel instantly better. I let out an audible sigh of relief.

"Is it that bad?" Paul asks. "Being here with me?"

I blink up at him, surprised. "What? No. It's not that."

He hands me the glass of water and I chug down half of it in mighty gulps.

"Then what's wrong?"

I start speaking before I've gathered my thoughts. "I'm just not used to all this glitz and glamour, and I feel like a fraud, somehow. Being here."

"I thought it would be fun. A nice change from what we're used to."

"Oh, of course. I know. It will be. I just need a minute."

I guess I wasn't very convincing, 'cause Paul takes my free hand and squeezes it. "We don't have to stay here. We can go anywhere. I'll take you wherever you want to go."

"Really?" And I smile for what might be the first time tonight. "Do you mean it?"

"Of course I do. I hate to see you this uncomfortable. Where do you want to go?"

It don't take me but a split second to decide where I'd rather be.

"I wanna go home." But I don't mean home to Maynardville. I mean home to the Burnett farm, where Laura is probably makin' snow ice cream just like me and Mama used to make, and Granny and Pawpaw are playing dominoes, and

Sadie is keeping Mrs. Burnett company while all the men are finishing up their work for the night, and the house smells like ham and biscuits, and the fire's going and the living room is cozy, and the radio is playing Bing Crosby. And it feels like family. Not a bunch of strangers in gowns and gloves. And it ain't about Paul at all. I may have come here for him, but I'm stayin' for his family.

33

The Kiss

Days later, I'm still reeling from what may have been the best worst New Year's ever. I remember every detail and I've been trying to put it in a letter for Margaret Ann.

Paul had brought me home as soon as I asked, and back at the Burnett farm, the family atmosphere hugged me tight. I got outa that fancy dress and into some overalls and cozy socks. Laura and Sadie had brought Mrs. Burnett out to the living room, and everyone played cards and dominoes and ate corn bread and black-eyed peas.

Paul and I had been the only ones who stayed awake until the clock struck midnight. We were sitting on the front porch swing, wrapped up in a blanket. I finally got an answer to the question I had asked the day before: "When I was here workin' on the farm, and you did all them nice things for me. Did you have feelings for me?"

He had fidgeted and looked around like he was searching for an answer. "June," he finally said, "when I found you, it was like a gift was given to me. To my family. You lit up the whole of Lafayette. You came to us at a time when we really needed something good in our lives. And you reminded all of us so much of Claire."

I remembered how devastated they all were by his cousin Claire's death just two years before.

"That's just one reason the whole family really took to you. And I did, too, for other reasons." He blushed after saying this. "But you were only fourteen."

Our conversation was interrupted by the sound of fireworks in the distance, and Paul looked at his watch. "It's midnight."

And this is the part that keeps runnin' through my head: He leaned in and kissed me right on the lips. I went numb.

With his mouth still on mine, he said, "Happy New Year."

All I could manage was, "Th-thanks you."

Thanks you? I'm tellin' you, that kiss turned me into a fuzzy-headed mess, and now I'm torn between wantin' to hide and wantin' to kiss him again. So I've been wandering around, bumpin' into things like a pinball, tryin' to do my chores without thinkin' about Paul, but it's no use. And I haven't been able to sit still long enough to write to Margaret Ann about it.

"You're certainly all smiles," Laura says one morning as she and Sadie are sizzlin' up sausages for breakfast.

I dance over to Little Jerry, in his highchair, and tickle his chin. His baby giggles are music to my ears. Then again, ever since that kiss, everything is music to my ears – even Sadie's judging sighs.

I grab my coat from the hook by the door, a silly smile still plastered on my face. "I'll be back. Goin' to see a man about some cows that need milkin'."

Sure enough, Paul's in the big barn when I get there, and my head goes fuzzy again.

"Got 'em started for you," he says, nodding toward the two he already milked.

"Gee, thanks. What would I ever do without you?" I shoot him a flirty grin.

Paul heaves himself off of the stool and steps toward me, removing his gloves. "Aww, I'm sure you'd survive just fine without me."

"I don't know about that." My flirtatious tone turns serious. "This place, this farm ... it's magic. I cain't imagine leavin'."

We sit down together on a stack of hay up against the wall, and I listen to the peacefulness of a winter morning on the Burnett farm. The occasional grunt of a cow, a rooster's wake-up call, wind chimes tinklin', the faraway hoot of an owl. It really is magic. It makes me forget everything else.

"Don't you miss home? Don't you need to go back to Maynardville?" Paul asks it like he's afraid of the answer.

I think on that a spell. "It's not home anymore. The bank's probably already taken the farm. My whole family's gone. I don't have anything left in Maynardville."

"You have me," a familiar voice says breathlessly from just outside the barn door.

I whip around, eyes wide, and standing there is Jimmy.

34

"My Girl"

"Jimmy!" I stand, and part of me wants to dash to him and fold myself into his arms, but then another part of me remembers our fight, so I don't know what to do. I walk hesitantly toward him, and up close, I search his eyes.

"June, I was so worried. Everybody has been." And he pulls me in and hugs me tight.

I sense Paul gettin' up to leave, and I think I hear him say, "I'll let you two catch up," and there's no kindness in his voice. "Don't forget about those cows."

"What are you doing here? How did you find me? How did you *get* here?" I'm so full of questions and don't know what to ask first.

Jimmy inches back so that we're lookin' face to face, and he grasps my hands. "I came to find you, of course. To bring you home. June, I'm so sorry about what I said. You know I didn't mean it the way it came out."

I shake my head, and suddenly tears are spilling out. "No, no, I'm sorry! I shouldn'ta slapped you, and I feel terrible about that. I was awful to you, and I didn't think you'd forgive me."

He caresses my cheeks in his hands. "How could I not forgive you? We belong together, remember?"

Emotions flood my body, and I feel like my heart's liable to explode. Of course we belong together, me and Jimmy. I had forgotten. In all my grief, all my anger, I had forgotten. And then ... Paul. And the kiss. I turn away from Jimmy.

"I have to milk the cows." I motion for him to follow me to the milking stool next to one of the eight cows in the barn. As I situate myself and get started, Jimmy perches on a railing. I look up at him, wondering if he can read my eyes. "So tell me how you found me, and how you got here."

"I, uh, I had a lot of help, let's just say that. From the Porters, from Margaret Ann, from the postmaster. And from my uncle."

I stop milkin' and sit up straight. "Your uncle. The hobo uncle?"

He nods.

"You mean— did you—"

"I did. Once I figured out where you were, I hopped the next train coming this way. There's something important I need to tell you, June. You're not gonna believe this—"

We turn and look when we hear Paul coming back into the barn. He steps up behind me and squeezes my shoulder. "Breakfast is ready. You can finish this later." Then he turns to Jimmy. "When are you leaving?"

Jimmy stands like he's accepted a challenge, so I spring up between them. "He's stayin' for breakfast, Paul. If that's okay?"

Paul slaps the gloves in his hand against his leg and purses his lips. "Sure. I guess." And he turns to leave.

When I look at Jimmy, his eyes are on fire. "Glad to see

you didn't kill him, but is there anything you need to tell me?"

My throat closes up, and all the things I need to tell him are spinning around in my mind, but I shake my head.

Everyone's seated at the table – except Paul, who's making up a plate for Mrs. Burnett – and all heads turn to look at us when we walk into the kitchen.

"Everyone, June has a visitor," Paul says. "This is …" and he looks at me expectantly.

"This is Jimmy. We grew up together." I smile and scoot Jimmy toward a seat without making eye contact with anybody.

But Jimmy interjects, "June's my girl." He grabs my hand and adds, "I've come to take her home to Maynardville."

Paul gives Jimmy a glare that could truly kill, and then leaves the room in a hurry. The others glance at each other, confused – except Sadie, who's clearly delighted by this turn of events.

Mr. Burnett extends a hand. "Well, welcome, Jimmy. Any friend of June's is a friend of ours. Long as you don't eat too much." And the comic relief eases the palpable tension.

Breakfast is quieter than usual, and I busy myself makin' up things that Little Jerry needs help with. Every so often, Jimmy asks a question, and either Laura or Mr. Burnett answers it. And every so often, Jimmy compliments the food and thanks the family for their generosity.

Then Laura asks, "How long you in town for?"

Jimmy wipes his mouth with a napkin, then looks at me. "Hopefully not long. How long will it take you to get ready?"

I'm frazzled. This is all so fast. I wasn't plannin' on leavin' here. Mrs. Burnett needs me. The family needs me. No one needs me in Maynardville. But I cain't talk about all that now, in front of everybody. I feel my face warm up, and under my clothes I'm sweating, never mind that it's thirty degrees outside.

Laura sees my discomfort and says, "There's no rush. Jimmy, you can stay here as long as y'all need. I think June has some unfinished business here."

Sadie gets up from the table, and I can barely hear, but I'm pretty sure she says, "Isn't that the understatement of the year?"

Mr. Burnett gets up too, and says, "Paul has plenty of room in the guest house. You can stay with him. But I may put you to work." And with that, the table's gettin' cleared and dishes are gettin' done, and I know I need to help out, but I also know I need to talk to Jimmy. Especially before he goes to stay with Paul in the guest house.

35

Where I Belong

"It's complicated, Jimmy." We're on the second-floor porch. The porch that Paul and I call *ours*. "I lost my whole family. Home isn't *home* anymore. I feel at home here. On the Burnett farm."

He looks away from me, stares out at the mountains, and I wait for him to respond. He finally turns to me, disbelief on his face. "How can you say that? Maynardville *is* your home. The farm—"

"The farm that I'm probably gonna lose," I interrupt.

Jimmy shifts to the edge of his chair. "No, June! That's what I needed to tell you. You're not losing the farm. Pastor Klein took up a collection. Everybody in Maynardville, practically, donated. It turns out there wasn't a whole lot left on the mortgage, and the money the pastor collected will pay a lot of it. It's yours."

I'm completely stunned. My mouth hangs open like Sadie's when I called her an old spinster. It's mine. *Mine*. I can live there with Molly and Bug and the chickens, and I can visit

Josy and Daddy and Mama under the pawpaw trees anytime I want. And I can be with Jimmy.

I cain't hide my smile. And I cain't believe the whole town did that for me. My gratitude comes out in tears, and I shake my head. "This is incredible."

"I know it won't be the same there without..." he doesn't say *without everyone you loved 'cause they're all dead now.* "But we can get through this. I'll be there for you. If you'll have me."

I cain't speak, or breathe. I can only stare and taste the salt on my tongue. Jimmy leans over and embraces me gently, hesitantly, like he's afraid to hurt me.

Finally, I make my voice work. "I need time."

Jimmy leans back in his chair and his shoulders drop. "What is it about this place? What's keeping you here?"

I sigh and gather my thoughts. "These people ... they're like family. I love them."

"And Paul? Didn't he kill your brother?"

I realize then that Jimmy doesn't know the whole story. "No! No, he didn't. I learned that he was there, but he wasn't the one who beat up Josy. In fact, Paul made an effort to get the man arrested who did. He's in jail now, that man, thanks to Paul."

"And you believe his story?" Jimmy squints his eyes.

A sudden rush of doubt hits me like a freight train. I hadn't even questioned Paul's story. I just took it at face value. There was an article in the paper. I read it, I saw the picture of Jeff Donahue, I saw Paul's face, his eyes.

"Yes," I reply now with certainty. "Yes, I believe him."

"And? Do you love him?"

Even though I knew this question was coming, it's a shock hearing it asked. "The feelings I had for him before ... those feelings did come back."

As scared as I am, I watch Jimmy's face for a reaction, and it hurts so badly to see the pain in his eyes.

The next time I see Jimmy, Mr. Burnett is takin' him around the farm, showin' him what all needs to be done. They're composting and preparing seeds so they'll be ready for spring planting, and Mr. Burnett keeps sayin' that Jimmy came just in time. "My best farmhand quit on me," he says, "so we need all the help we can get."

While I wash the clothes on the back porch, I think about what I'm going to do. I never woulda thought I'd be considering staying in Lafayette with the railroad bull I thought had killed Josy. And now it's hard to believe that I'm not immediately runnin' back home with Jimmy. What in the world is my problem?

The next garment I pull out of the basket beside my feet is a shirt of Paul's. I've seen him wear it a few times. It's plaid with about twenty shades of blue, except for a stain on one sleeve, just about at the elbow. I dip it into the bucket of soapy water, then flatten it over the washboard. I scrub the stained sleeve with a bar of soap, then rub the shirt against the washboard's grooves. It feels intimate, touching Paul's clothing, like I'm listening in on a secret conversation, one that he'd be embarrassed for me to hear.

"You're gonna have to scrub harder if you want to get all the dirt out." Paul comes up the porch steps, seemingly out of nowhere. *How does he do that?* He sets himself into a chair a few feet away and eyes me warily.

I quickly wring the shirt out and hang it up on the

clothesline that stretches across the back porch, feeling his eyes on me.

"When were you gonna tell me?" he asks. "About you being 'Jimmy's girl'?"

I expect to see anger on his face, but all I see is hurt.

"I thought he hated me. We had a big fight before I left, and I thought it was over. He surprised me, comin' here."

Paul stands and closes the space between us, and despite the January cold, I feel the heat comin' off him. "Well, in case you forget where you belong," he says, and with gentle hands, he pulls my head up 'til our lips meet.

36

Baby Steps

I cain't decide if I'd like to be a fly on the wall in the guest house or not, watchin' how Paul and Jimmy get along. Or how they don't.

It's clear to me that Jimmy's not leavin' here without me, and Paul ain't goin' nowhere, so it's all up to me. I have to choose – Lafayette, where the Burnett family has given me a home, and where Paul can give me a new life, or Maynardville, the only home I've ever really known, where I grew up, where Jimmy, the love of my life, is, and where my real family lie in rest under the pawpaw trees.

The pressure is maddening, and them boys seem to be doin' all they can to make it harder to figure things out.

Like that kiss, and what Paul said. *In case you forget where you belong.* If I knew where I belong, I wouldn't be in this mess, now, would I? And besides that, who is he to tell me where I belong, like I belong to him?

Part of me is appalled at his arrogance, but another part melts like butter on a hotplate just thinkin' about that kiss. And it only gets worse.

One day, Jimmy practically prances into the smokehouse with a deer straddling his shoulders. "Got us some venison that'll last the rest of the winter, I'll bet."

Then Jimmy and Paul spend the afternoon arguing about the best way to skin it, bone it, and trim it. They even argue about how much the thing weighs.

The next day, Paul surprises me with a caramel cube at lunchtime, so Jimmy goes off to town and comes back with a whole handful of 'em. Not to be outdone, Paul starts leavin' caramel cubes in the laundry like he used to, on our upstairs porch, in the barn by the milking supplies, by my bedroom door, and gosh darn, I never thought it would happen, but I'm about sick to death of caramel cubes now. And when Jimmy catches wind of Paul's gifts, I glimpse him a time or two trying to sneak the caramel cubes away before I find 'em.

The worst part is when the two of them boys (and I do mean boys) are in the same room trying to puff out their feathers for me, like that male purple martin. Today it goes like this: Paul puts his arm out to help me up the porch steps, and Jimmy runs up to my other side and grabs my arm, and then I've got both of them practically lifting me up the steps like I'm some kinda invalid.

"Stop it!" I shake them off and stomp across the porch. "You two are bein' ridiculous! I know how to walk up some steps."

Their mouths drop and they look dumbfounded, but a split second later, they turn on each other.

"I was here first!" Paul yells.

"No," Jimmy says sternly, "I've been here for June for ten years."

I leave before I can hear any more of their nonsense.

I try to stay focused on why I'm here – to help Mrs. Burnett and the family while she's sick. She's taken a turn for the worse and needs more help sittin' up and eatin' and takin' her medications and whatnot. For most of that, I'm lettin' her family step in, and I'm takin' over other things so they can spend more time with her.

I've become a pro at changin' Little Jerry's diapers, givin' him his bottle, and playin' with him, that's for sure.

Sittin' in the living room on a blanket with Little Jerry is my favorite thing to do now. We dump out his basket of toys, and he squeals and laughs, and so do I. As I'm makin' his favorite stuffed elephant "talk" in my best elephant voice, Little Jerry reaches for the coffee table, clamps his little hands on the edge, and pulls himself up. And just like he's been plannin' to do this for months, he turns and waddles toward me, takin' three gangly steps before fallin' forward into my lap.

"Oh my gosh! Little Jerry, you walked!" I call for Laura. "Laura! Come quick!"

Before I know it, everybody within earshot is gathered around, and I help Little Jerry to his feet and tell Laura to call him over to her. As we watch, as God is my witness, this perfect little baby step-step-steps over to his mama, and the whole room erupts in cheers. And it's not Paul my eyes seek out amidst the celebration. It's Jimmy. It's always been Jimmy.

I go to bed that night thinkin' about Little Jerry's first steps. How they were awkward but determined, careful but risky. And that reminds me of how Jimmy told me once that I'm full of contradictions. That's life, though, isn't it? We go about our ups and downs, our adventures and our sorrows, our risks and our failures, taking baby steps. Learning as we go.

I don't know why it took that one little moment –

watching the baby walk for the first time and feeling my eyes flick automatically to Jimmy – to realize what I should have known all along.

I think it will take baby steps for me to learn to live again at home in Maynardville, but I'm sure now that home in Maynardville is where I really belong. This family in Lafayette – they've been so good to me, but I cain't go on pretending that they're family. I need to rejoin *my* family on *my* farm in Maynardville.

Now that I've made that decision, I cain't wait to wake up in the morning and tell Jimmy, whose heart I surely must have broken by telling him I have feelings for Paul.

37

There's No Time

I stand on the upstairs porch, watchin' a hawk soar above the trees on a gorgeous January morning, snow falling gently and silently onto the hills. Hawks are thought to be messengers from Heaven, so I imagine it's coming to tell me about Mama and Daddy and Josy. And I consider it a sign that I've made the right decision about going home. This spurs me to go find Jimmy to let him know.

After I'm all freshened up and dressed, I hear someone holler downstairs, and the noise gets louder as I descend. It's coming from Mrs. Burnett's room.

When I turn the corner into her room, Mr. Burnett, Granny and Pawpaw, Laura and her husband, and Sadie are all in there, and immediately I know something's wrong.

I push through to Mrs. Burnett's bed, and I'm shocked to see how much worse she looks than just yesterday. Her face is as gray and ashen as her hair, which is matted to her face in sweaty strings. Her lips are dry and cracked, cheeks gaunt, shoulders shaking, and she's groaning – a low, sad sound just like Josy on his last day.

I look up at Laura, and she pulls me into a hug and whispers, "Paul needs to come say goodbye. Can you run find him?"

"But—"

"Don't argue. There's no time."

I back out of the room, disbelieving, then turn and run out onto the porch to see Paul and Jimmy in fisticuffs, rolling around on the cold ground.

"Paul!"

Either they sense the urgency in my voice, or they notice whose name I call and whose name I don't, but they quickly roll to a stop and look up, brown grass blades and snow in their hair and on their coats.

"It's M—"

I cain't say it, but I point, lips quivering, toward the hallway, and Paul knows. He clambers up, runs and stumbles up the steps and into the house, and I just stand there lookin' at Jimmy. His face is blotchy and red and there's a bruise blooming on his brow.

He stands, brushes himself off, steps toward me, and I feel my face crumple as I sink into his arms.

The doctor comes a few minutes later, and he says it's time. But Mrs. Burnett told me she was supposed to have a few more months. I've only been here a couple of weeks. I cain't help but think I bring death to anyone I love, and I know that sounds awful, but that's where my mind goes.

"June," Jimmy asks, lifting my chin to look in my eyes, "are you gonna be alright?"

I nod. "I decided I need to go home with you. To Maynardville. But now…"

"You need to be here for the Burnetts. I understand. We'll stay and help with whatever they need."

That's when I know it for sure. "I love you, Jimmy."

He pulls me close, puts his cheek on mine, and caresses my head. "I love you too, June. We have all the time in the world. Together."

38

No Good With Goodbyes

The next few days pass in a blur. The whole Burnett family is crushed under the weight of the thickest haze of grief. At the same time, they're blowing around like tumbleweeds, fetching the coroner, making arrangements, settling debts, cleaning the sick room, dressing the casket, digging the burial plot, choosing the prayers and the hymns, notifying friends and family, and all the things that go into bidding farewell to a loved one.

I've had my share of tragic farewells, so I spend my time hidden in the barn, with or without the cows. I sit alone with my grief because I cain't face Laura, cain't see the devastation on her face. I cain't face Mr. Burnett, who I know is weeping for the first time in his life. I cain't face Sadie, whose scolding eyes are now weak and dejected. I cain't face Granny and Pawpaw, who expected to be buried long before their daughter.

And I cain't face Paul, especially, because I know I need to tell him that I'm leaving. That it's not him I was ever in love with. It's this family, this farm, that reminds me so much of how life used to be in Maynardville, before the Devil touched the earth and turned everything to dust. Back when we were happy and sittin' on top of the world. Before everyone I held dear was buried under the pawpaw trees.

We stay for the service, Jimmy by my side the entire time, holding me up. Mr. Burnett had asked me to write something for the funeral, but I just couldn't. Guilt gnaws at me relentlessly for that. Thank God the family understands. They know I've been through too much grief.

We stay for several days after, helping with the cooking and cleaning that others are too grieved to bother with. We tend to the animals, we gather the eggs, we haul food from the cellar, we clean and replenish the wood stove.

It's Paul who approaches me in the barn one day. "Can we talk?"

Jimmy says he'll give us some privacy, squeezes my hands, and steps out. Paul motions to the stacks of hay by the wall, and we sit, both of us red-eyed and tired.

"I want to thank you," he says. "You and Jimmy. For all that you've done to help our family during all of this. You didn't have to."

"Yes, I did."

Paul shakes his head. "Listen, what I want to say is, well…" He searches for words. "I think I can see that you have made a decision."

I search his face, and I don't see hurt. Maybe resignation. I decide to be completely honest. "I have. I need to go home to Maynardville. And I love Jimmy." I look down, fidget with some hay.

"You don't have to feel bad, June, you really don't."

I look up at him, and both our eyes are watery again. "I'm

sorry—"

"No, don't be sorry. It's pretty clear you belong with Jimmy. You two have a history. A good one, not like ours," he chuckles. "And ... I guess if I have to lose, I'm okay with losin' to a guy like him."

"I'm sorry," I say again, embarrassed. And I truly am sorry. I don't like the thought of anyone feelin' hurt.

He puts a hand up. "Look, when it's love, it's love."

"Are you terribly upset?"

Paul's eyes go to the rafters, then he blows out an exasperated sigh. "If I'm being honest, I think I knew all along that you would need to return to Maynardville. That your journey wasn't over."

I think on that a spell. "That's a nice way to think of it. A journey. It's been a tough one, but you're right, it's not over. I *am* needed at home."

"Of course you are. And if you ever want to come back and visit, you will always be welcome."

Jimmy and I pack up our things, and Laura fills my bag with some leftovers after lunch, our last meal with the Burnetts.

I'm no good with goodbyes. I usually just leave a note and take off when no one's lookin', so this extended goodbye is incredibly difficult. And having just lost Mrs. Burnett makes it even harder.

I hold onto Little Jerry's chubby little legs and blow raspberries on his belly as he giggles and giggles, and I'm gigglin' too, except there are tears streamin' down my face.

I hug Granny and Pawpaw's necks, and they smile kindly and nod like they think I'm just goin' out for a bit and will be right back.

Mr. Burnett tells me and Jimmy that we got a job here anytime, anytime indeed, and it kills me that his big, gruff voice has lost all of its power.

Laura is cryin' before I even get to her, and she leaves her husband's arms and falls into mine. "I will miss you so much. But I wish you all the best, I really do. You deserve it."

I cain't find the words, like so many other times in my life, so I'm smiling and blubbering, but I don't want to miss my chance to say the things I want to say. "I love you. And I will write to you." And I pull myself away from her before I can change my mind.

There's a chorus of goodbyes and waves, and Jimmy and I start our trek down the drive. Before we get to the end, I hear my name and footsteps runnin' behind us, and I turn around. It's Sadie.

"June, wait." She catches up, and then she's standing there in front of me, the anger gone from her eyes. "Thank you. For everything. You've been a real help here." Then she nods toward Jimmy and says, "You too. Thank you."

I smile and nod. "Take care, Sadie."

And we walk away, toward home.

39

Uncle Charlie

Jimmy says we're going to one of his uncle's camps and hoppin' a train from there. I let him lead me every step of the way. I'm a contradiction again: more broken than ever, but excited about what's to come.

It's nearly sundown by the time we get to the camp, and I plop down against a tree and bring my knees up and bury my head, letting the tears dampen my coat sleeves. Tears for Mrs. Burnett and for what I'm leaving behind.

When I finally lift my head, Jimmy is a few trees over, sitting on an upturned bucket next to a firepit with a hobo. Their voices carry over to me, and the hobo's voice sounds familiar. I get up, and as I approach them, the firelight shines on the man's face, and – oh my word, I know who that is, but it cain't be!

"June, this is my Uncle Charlie," Jimmy says when I reach them.

"Charlie? Oh my Lord, Charlie! Is it really you?" I'm practically jumping up and down as Charlie nods, a smile spreading across his lined face.

Jimmy stutters, confused.

"Charlie was one of Josy's friends on the rails! He and Pate took care of Josy, and he's been to the house loads of times. I cain't believe this is the uncle you've been talkin' about!" I turn to Charlie. "Me and Pate thought for sure you were dead."

Charlie's eyes light up. "You seen young Pate? I thought he didn't make it past the bulls."

"He did!" I kneel down next to Charlie, aware of the angry looks I'm gettin' from hobos who are tryin' to sleep. "He's workin' at an auto shop in Memphis. I just saw him before Christmas."

"Mighty glad to hear it. Mighty glad to hear it."

Charlie and Jimmy are shakin' their heads like it's a small world with big coincidences.

"And how're your folks, June?"

My face falls, and Jimmy takes the lead. "They've passed, Uncle Charlie."

We sit in silence a bit, orange flames lighting up the sorrow in Charlie's face. It's quiet, save for the low hum of some hobos snorin' and some talkin' about the weather, the trains, their aching backs. Charlie shares some stew with us, and we slurp hungrily.

"Charlie, how come you didn't tell us you got kin in Maynardville when you came to our house with Josy?"

"Well, Mr. and Mrs. Mackenroe ain't keen on my life choices," he says matter of factly.

"My mother and father say he's not part of the family," Jimmy adds. "They don't want me hanging around him, or even talkin' to him."

"So when I came to town with Joseph that first time," Charlie explains, "I thought I might be able to see Jimmy, but …"

"I honestly had no idea he was ever in town," Jimmy says. "I'm glad you got to meet the Bakers, Uncle Charlie. They were real good people."

His sincerity is tempered with resentment and anger at his parents for keeping him from his uncle. I cain't understand why Jimmy's parents would do that. Charlie's a real good man.

Now I see a different side of things. "So, Jimmy, when you told me about your uncle, back before I went train hoppin', and you gave me all those tips and things … you were taking a big risk, weren't you? I mean, if your folks had heard you, what would've happened?"

Jimmy shrugged. "I just wanted to help. Besides, they ain't ever home. Even when they are."

That hits me hard in the gut. *Even when they are.* I've seen Jimmy practically raise himself, fend for himself, but I've never understood why. And talk about a contradiction – his folks hardly care what he's doin' day to day, but they won't let him talk to his uncle? I mark this on my mental list of things I need to talk to Jimmy more about. But now is not the time.

I fill Charlie in on all the things that happened after I last saw him – my train hopping adventure dressed as a boy, my finding Paul and working on his farm, then finding Pate, then finding out that Paul killed Josy, then what happened to Daddy, then Mama, and finding out Paul *didn't* kill Josy.

It takes nearly an hour to relay the whole story, even though I leave out a lot of things, like workin' at the clothes factory with Mama, drivin' a car, the tornado, gettin' electricity at the farm, and gettin' a telephone. And before we even get to think about sleepin', the train's here, and Charlie agrees to come with us.

"Are you gonna miss Lafayette and the Burnett farm?" Jimmy asks me when we're as settled as we can be in the corner of an almost empty train car.

I don't have to think on that for a second. "I will. I will miss the way it was, before. Mrs. Burnett was the glue … and without her, the whole thing falls apart."

"What whole thing?"

"The fantasy, I guess. The fantasy of one big, happy family."

"But what about at home?" Jimmy shifts uncomfortably in the dark boxcar. "At home, there's no Mrs. Burnett."

"Well, at home I was the glue. So the way I see it, I can hold everything together, or let it fall apart."

We lock eyes, and at the same time, we say, "Hold it together."

Jimmy takes my hand in his. "Together," he says.

40

Normal Ol' June

Coming back to Maynardville, walking up that hill that leads us into town, my heart swells, and a sob pours out. I quietly apologize to my home for even thinking of not coming back.

The urge to stop in at all the shops is great, but we walk straight on through to the lane and all the way down to my farm. The barn, the chicken coop that Jimmy painted, the wood shed, the cellar, the house – everything looks the same as I last saw it, except empty. I don't know why I'm surprised. It's only been about a month since I left town.

I think I was afraid to come back because I felt like I had nothing left here. I was afraid to be here without Mama. I turn and walk toward the pawpaw trees, three wooden crosses standing tall beneath them. I kneel down in front of them, brush away some dirt, pull a weed growing close to one of the crosses, and I sit with them. My family. Josy, Daddy, Mama – the order they were buried here.

I sit with them, and for the first time, I don't feel a crushing sorrow, but a determination, a responsibility. I promise them I will be here for them and take care of them as long as I live.

When I go back to school, everybody handles me with kid gloves, Jimmy especially. I don't mind it comin' from him, 'cause I know his heart. It's when all the other kids do it that it puts me on edge. I just want to be normal for once.

So one day when I've had enough of the whispers and pitiful glances and everyone bein' afraid to talk to me, I approach Miss Glass at lunch break.

"What's bothering you, June?" she asks, putting down her sandwich.

"Well, I want people to stop actin' all strange around me. They don't want to talk to me, they won't make eye contact with me, and I know they're all talkin' about me. Well, Bertha Bellows talks about everyone, but even the nice kids are doin' it now."

Miss Glass suppresses a smile and leans back in her chair. Her glasses rest thoughtfully on her nose, and her eyes twinkle with knowledge that I'm praying to tap into.

"Imagine if one of those nice kids were out of school for a while, and you found out that she had an unbearable amount of tragedy in her life," Miss Glass says. "What would you say to her when she returned to school?"

I think on that a spell. "I think I would let her know that I care about her, but then I would just treat her normally, like always."

"That's good, June. Maybe your classmates don't know what they're supposed to say or do."

"Hmm. Would it be alright if I tell them? I could write an essay and present it to the class."

Miss Glass smiles. "Why, June, I think that's a fine idea. Hand your essay in to me tomorrow, and we'll set a time for you to present it next week."

I'm walkin' on air when I go out into the yard to eat my lunch, and I spend the rest of the day thinkin' about what I'm going to say.

The day of my presentation, I stand at the front of the room and clear my throat. I ain't nervous one bit, 'cause I'm so tired of bein' "the girl who lost her whole family," and I'm ready to set things straight.

"Your essay is profound," Miss Glass had told me after she'd read it, "and I think your classmates will appreciate hearing it."

Now all eyes are watching me with caution, probably wondering if I'm going to cry. I'm determined not to, but you never know these days.

"I know you all are wondering what you're supposed to say to me or how you're supposed to act around me since I lost my brother, my daddy, and then my mama. I understand how you must feel, so today I'd like to tell you some things you can say and do."

I let out a sharp breath, then continue. "You can ask me how I'm doing, and then don't be afraid to hear the answer. I'll try real hard not to cry on your shoulder too often."

I smile, and the ice is broken. I'm thrilled to see the whole class relax and laugh a little.

"You can tell me about what's going on in your lives. A good person once told me *we all have our tragedies.* Your problems are just as important as mine, so let me hear about them."

Miss Glass beams at me, and my friends look at one another and nod.

"And, well, just treat me like a normal girl, like you've

always done. Nancy, you can pinch me on St. Patrick's Day if you want. Barbara, you can snatch my biscuits any time you want. George, you can whistle at me – just watch out for Jimmy."

By now, the whole class is laughin', and so am I.

"And Luke, you can even pull my braids if you want to. The point is, even though I have a big hole in my heart now, I'm still normal ol' June."

Everyone stands and claps, and then Nancy, Barbara, and even Bertha come and hug me, and it takes a while 'fore Miss Glass gets us all settled down to learn about Amelia Earhart.

And now I'm more inspired than ever. Who would have thought that a woman would be flying across any ocean, let alone doing it solo? Miss Glass says the world has opened up for women because of Amelia Earhart. She says Opportunity is knocking, and we have to be brave enough to open the door.

Now, as I look around at my classmates, who are more understanding and comfortable with me because of my speech, I feel good about myself and excited for the future. I vow to always open the door when Opportunity is there. And not just open it – step out and embrace it.

41

A Wedding to Remember

M iss Glass's wedding is a whole-town affair. She'd caused a
stir for wantin' to have it in the school house instead of the
church, in honor of her family before her who built the school.
But after a while, people started to warm up to the idea, and
before long, all of Maynardville was involved in gettin'
everything ready.

There's a good reason for that, too. It turns out that Miss
Glass's wedding is also a farewell. She's marrying Mr. Wayne
Parsons, who just joined the Army. He's gonna be stationed in
Fort Knox, Kentucky, so they're movin' there after the
wedding to live on the base. They're not even gettin' a
honeymoon. Miss Glass says the government's real concerned
about some man named Hitler in Germany, so our military's
gettin' ready. For what, I don't know, but I sure hope Miss
Glass's new husband don't have to go to war.

Anyway, since they ain't gonna get a honeymoon,
everybody in Maynardville decided we'd bring the honeymoon
to them. And that's how I come to spend three whole days

before the wedding decorating the school house in handmade Hawaiian leis, hibiscus flowers, and grass skirts. We even make some tiki torches, and we carve out some coconuts to use for butter mint bowls.

While the school house is transformed into a Hawaiian luau, Miss Glass is transformed into an absolute goddess. Her dark hair, usually knotted up in a bun or pinned back in a braid, flows freely down her back. Gone are the horn-rimmed glasses and the stern teacher look. Instead, she's made up in mascara and powder and coral lipstick, and a sequined veil waves over her head. If I didn't already know that was Miss Glass, I would mistake her for a glamorous movie star.

Mrs. Tomlinson plays the piano, which someone somehow squeezed into a corner of the room. Miss Glass's fiancé stands bashfully and pink-cheeked at the front, next to Pastor Klein, and when the wedding march starts and Miss Glass emerges, the whole audience stands and oohs and aahs. They're so enthralled they don't even seem to mind that they've been sittin' in little ol' student desks.

We watch her float down the aisle, this unbelievably fancy lady who looks so different from the usual strict but fun-loving teacher we all know and love. When she spots me, she lifts her poofy dress at the hem and wiggles a foot at me – Hawaiian print wedge sandals! She winks and smiles and continues her slow glide toward her future husband.

Now I'm beaming just as brightly as the bride. I've never been to a wedding before, but I think this one is exactly how I would want mine to be.

After the I-dos and the I-wills and the 'til-death-do-us-parts, the whole crowd moves out into the spring sunshine and we celebrate and mourn at the same time. Miss Glass has been our teacher since I was a pup, and I cain't imagine her not bein' here no more. Everybody else in Maynardville feels the same way – even ol' Bertha Bellows, who talks bad about people behind their backs.

When everybody else in the whole world has had their time with the bride and groom, Miss Glass – er, Mrs. Parsons – finally comes over to me. I'm sittin' at a picnic table with Jimmy and a few kids from school, enjoying some pineapple punch and coconut sugar cookies. Miss Glass – *aw, crumbs, I ain't never gonna get used to callin' her by any other name* – has a big smile on her face. Even after all this to-do, she don't look weary.

"Children, I want you to meet your new teacher, Ms. Randolph. She's just over there." And as soon as she motions, a woman steps up next to her, and I'll be a tiger with no stripes! It's Mama Helen!

"I know you!" we both say at the same time. The others are flabbergasted when Mama Helen (I'm gonna have to get used to callin' her Mrs. Randolph) and I embrace, and she says, "I'm so glad to see that you've got a sparkle in your eyes."

Then we have to explain to everybody how we know each other, and ain't it such a small world?

"Just goes to show, the Lord puts people in your path for a reason," Helen says.

Thinkin' back on how she watched out for me in Nashville and helped me get a coat and somethin' to eat, and how she gave me a nickel to call Margaret Ann even though she hardly had two to rub together, I know she's going to be the perfect replacement for Miss Glass for my last year of school next fall.

Turns out Mama Helen has family in Maynardville, and she moved here for help with bringin' up her kids. "It's also less expensive here than in the Nashville area," she says.

Whatever the reason, I'm over the moon, 'cause I didn't

think I'd ever get to see Mama Helen again or thank her for her kindness. I decide I'll keep to myself who she reminds me of and what I'm callin' her in my head – at least for now.

42

Orchestra

June 1935

"Uncle Charlie, let's go," Jimmy yells. "We don't wanna be late."

He tosses a basket packed with fried chicken, potato salad, and soda pop into the wagon, then jumps up into the seat next to me and takes Molly's reins.

Charlie finally trots down the porch steps and squeezes in on the other side of me. "The festival ain't goin' nowhere, just hold your horses," he says. "Or your mule." We laugh as we clomp down the drive and up the lane to Maynardville.

The field by the old Macafee's general store has been transformed. Lining the perimeter are picnic tables piled with fruit and cakes and sausages and grilled corn and I-don't-know-what-all. In between those tables are more tables with games and crafts for the little ones, with prizes like candy and pinwheels and paper flowers. And in between those tables are even more tables for folks sellin' their wares, like peach preserves and syrupy golden honey, homemade candles and quilted potholders.

Once we've parked the wagon and hopped down, Jimmy slips behind me and reaches around to cover my eyes. "There's a surprise for you, June. No peekin', now."

I squeal as he shuffles me along toward who-knows-where. "Where are you takin' me?"

"Almost there, almost there."

Then he's positioning me in the direction he wants me to face, and he says, "Okay, you ready? One, two …" and he takes his hands off my eyes, "three."

I blink a couple times, and in front of me is Mrs. Porter, and she's standing behind a table that's covered with bottles of herbs and tonics and whatnot – these are Mama's and my bottles. Then my eyes go to a banner stretched across the front of the table that says, "MAMA'S REMEDIES."

"What's this?" I ask, amazement in my eyes.

"This is your business, June, in honor of your mama, God rest her soul," Mrs. Porter says, "and you've already made ten sales this morning." Her smile is a mile long.

"Oh my goodness! I cain't—you did this for me?"

"With Jimmy's help," she says. "But really, you did this yourself. You and your dear mother."

"What do you think?" Jimmy asks.

"I'm speechless. I cain't thank y'all enough." And it's true. For once in my life, words are not comin' out of my mouth, 'cause there aren't enough words in the world to express how much this means to me. And what it means for my future. I just wish Mama could be here to see it. *The next big thing.*

As if she read my mind, Mrs. Porter says, "She'd be real proud of you, hon. And I know she's watchin' from Heaven."

"Thank you, Mrs. Porter."

She steps around the table and squeezes my shoulders. "I wouldn't have it any other way. And look. Your friends are here."

I follow her pointing finger, and there they are, just like they promised.

"Margaret Ann! Say-Lynn!"

We close the distance quickly, Margaret Ann squealin' that they're so lucky their mama allowed them to come. Then Jimmy says he's got a surprise for Uncle Charlie and we all gotta go back to the wagon. I turn to Mrs. Porter, and she says, "I got things covered here, now, y'all go explore."

At the wagon, I don't see nothin' special, and we're all standin' there waitin' for who-knows-what, and Jimmy says, "Any minute now."

"Any minute now what?" I ask.

Then all heads turn because right at that moment, walkin' up the road is none other than Pate! Charlie does a double-take, and even though I feel compelled to run to Pate, I stay back. This is a blessed reunion for Pate and Charlie, who each thought the other was dead for over a year.

We watch as they embrace and pat each other on the back and wipe their eyes, and before long, we're wipin' our eyes too. Then they beckon us over, and we join their reunion. Pate says he ought not to stay, and Uncle Charlie agrees.

"There ain't enough folks who are as accepting as you all," Charlie says, noddin' toward me and Jimmy.

"But you came all this way," I protest. "Cain't you stay for a little bit? Maynardville folks are kind, ain't they?"

Pate shakes his head. "They can be kind and still not want me around. I gotta get back anyway. Work and all."

I'm sad to see Pate go, but boy was it worth it to see him and Charlie reunite. We give him our phone number, and we all vow to get together sometime soon. And as we head back to the festival grounds, I'm talkin' a mile a minute about Memphis and Beale Street, until we get caught up in all the festival excitement.

There's so much to see and so many people to say hello to. And in the center of it all is a real live Ferris wheel, which we waste no time in gettin' on. At the top, we throw our hands in the air and wave to the tiny people on the ground. Up here in the wind and sky, I feel like I'm sittin' on top of the world. I haven't felt that way in a long time. For the rest of the ride, I'm smilin' so much my cheeks hurt.

Afterward, we find a clown makin' cotton candy, and darned if that clown ain't Mr. Macafee himself! I get a smudge of white makeup on my shirt sleeves when I throw my arms around his neck. He gives us some cotton candy for free, 'cause "this whole festival is for our Junebug, ain't it?"

For me? "What do ya mean, Mr. Macafee?"

"Oh, you'll see soon enough. Y'all enjoy yourselves now." And he silly-walks toward some little kids who are pleased as punch to see a clown.

My heart is full, and after our delicious lunch, my belly is too.

Jimmy and I watch from a distance as Uncle Charlie approaches Jimmy's folks, and we hold our breath, try to imagine what they're sayin'. We see nods, and maybe smiles, but we're too far away to tell for sure. I turn back to Margaret Ann to answer about a million questions she has about my trip to Lafayette. I'm in the middle of tellin' her about the horrible accident on the train, with Barney, when Jimmy nudges me and wags his thumb toward his folks. We both smile as we see Uncle Charlie and Jimmy's parents shake hands in a friendly manner, and then they sit together at a table, and it looks like they're havin' pleasant conversation.

As the afternoon yawns into a glorious breezy evening, Mayor Tomlinson steps up onto a small stage in front of the Ferris wheel. We all turn our heads to watch, and the festival noises and laughter and music and chitchat die down.

"Friends and families of Maynardville, and all over Union County," he says to the largest crowd I've seen, "my, this is quite the turnout. I can't thank you enough. We know that times are tough and these are dark days for so many folks. Your generosity today is a reminder that, as our Pastor Klein would say, 'God is great, and God will provide.'"

There's clapping and *amens* all around before the mayor continues. "Now, let me get to the part you're all waiting for."

Mrs. Tomlinson rushes over and hands him a small piece of paper. He looks at it, eyes wide, and clears his throat. "June Baker, would you please join me up on the stage?"

I gasp in surprise, and my friends nudge me forward. "What's going on?" I mouth.

On the stage, Mayor Tomlinson puts an arm around me. "Today, thanks to this wonderful community, we have raised a whopping two hundred, fifty-seven dollars and ninety cents. I'll throw in an extra dime to make it fifty-eight."

Laughter and applause fill the air, and then the mayor turns to face me. "After your mother died, we collected some money for you so that you wouldn't lose your home here in Maynardville. But we felt that wasn't enough."

My eyebrows shoot up, and I've got questions in my eyes.

"This money raised today is for you, young June. And I

do believe it's enough to pay off your mortgage and your car, and perhaps you can set some aside for your new business, Mama's Remedies."

My hands go up to my mouth, and I'm all tingles as the crowd erupts in cheers. "Mama's Remedies, folks," the mayor says to the crowd. "Best herbs and natural remedies in all of Union County, and it all started with this young lady's mother, Mrs. Baker. Now our June will carry that torch, and may God bless her with success."

Mayor Tomlinson hugs me, and Jimmy, Margaret Ann, Say-Lynn, and Charlie hop up onto the stage and bury me in their arms.

Those cheers and whistles and claps play on in my head like an orchestra late into the night, until finally, Uncle Charlie turns out the lights and retires to his room, Jimmy to his, and I to mine. In my house on my farm in Maynardville, Tennessee, where my beloved family are cheering for me too, under the pawpaw trees.

I park the newly repaired car outside the post office, relieved to have completed this final task that's been naggin' at me since Mrs. Burnett's funeral service. I don't know what's taken me so long or why it was so hard to do. I remember every second of my time with the Burnett family, cherish every second, and have so much to say that shoulda been said before.

When I hand the letter to Mr. Willis, he squints at my writing. "What's that say, Missy? The name?"

"Oh, it's to Mr. Paul Burnett."

"It's thick," he says, squeezing the envelope. "Love letter?"

"Somethin' like that," I reply with a smile.

About the Author

Cheryl King is a born-and-raised Texan, Harry Potter fanatic, chocolate lover, and word nerd. By day, she is a dyslexia therapist. By night, she enjoys writing flash- and micro-fiction for contests like NYCMidnight and Writing Battle. She lives in Mansfield with her husband and two teen sons. She would love for you to review her books online.

Her debut novel, *Sitting on Top of the World*, is the first book in this duology.

Keep in touch

Learn more at CherylKingWritesThings.com.

Acknowledgments

Writing a book may seem like a solitary undertaking, but it is not done in isolation. I have many people to thank for making this sequel come to life.

To my husband, Chris, thanks for giving me the time, space, and encouragement to write.

Mom, your enthusiasm about my dreams helped make them come true.

Linda and Mike, thank you for believing in me.

Shelly, your history expertise was greatly appreciated.

Jamie, thank you for reading, supporting, and encouraging.

Thank you to beta readers Pat and Beth, and all of my newsletter subscribers.

Thank you to the team at 100Covers for creating a design that flows nicely from the first book.

Thank you to my critique group, 11:59 Workshop, for keeping me accountable to honing my craft.

And, most of all, thank you to you, dear reader, for taking a chance on an indie author and choosing my book from the shelf. Without you, there are no books.

Discussion Questions

1. How has June changed since the first book?

2. How does June's and Mama's grief affect their relationship?

3. Describe Jimmy and explain why June is drawn to him.

4. How is the tornado a metaphor for June's life?

5. In Chapter 7, Jimmy describes June in these words: "You're tough and strong, but also feminine and gentle. You're a rebel, but also a good, kindhearted person. You miss so much school, but you're smarter than anyone I know. You're soft and quiet, but you'll rip the head off of anyone that does you wrong." Share some examples of how June fits these descriptors.

6. Why doesn't June enjoy the Fourth of July picnic anymore?

7. Butterflies have a symbolic place in this book (the butterfly that lands on June, the bookmark from Jimmy, Mama's hairpin). Discuss this symbolism and the possible implications.

8. Like in the first book, trees also play an important role in this story (the pawpaw trees, the spindly tree that someone decorates for the holidays). Describe the importance of these trees and what they may symbolize.

9. Discuss how June's faith is shaken in Chapter 11.

10. In Chapter 13, Jimmy suggests there could be more to the story of Josy's beating by the railroad bulls. Do you think Josy may have instigated the fight, and if so, does that excuse the treatment he got?

11. Everyone June tells about her plan to kill Paul reacts in disbelief and tries to talk her out of it. Is June right to want revenge? Does Paul deserve punishment for his actions?

12. Pate has good reasons for not going with June on her mission. What does this tell you about his character? How might the story change if he went with her?

13. June may feel all alone at times, but she never really is. She has people along the way who help her. Discuss some of those interactions. How do they resemble real life for you?

14. What is the significance of June's dream in Chapter 23?

15. After learning more about Barney in Chapter 23, do you feel any differently about the accident? Do you think June feels differently?

16. In Chapter 24, Dan tells June to forgive Paul. What do you think about his advice? Is that something June is capable of?

17. Describe June's relationship with Mrs. Burnett. How has it changed since the first book?

18. What do you think of Paul's explanation about what happened with Josy? How should June react? Should she believe him?

19. Explain why June has such a hard time at the New Year's Eve party. What do you think it means that she wants to go home to the Burnett farm?

20. In Chapter 34, June faces the internal conflict of loving two boys: Jimmy and Paul. Discuss the pros and cons of each relationship.

21. In Chapter 37, how does June realize that it's Jimmy she really loves?

22. June has a history of not being able to handle goodbyes. In the first book, she developed a habit of leaving a note and taking off. In this book, she has had to deal with a number of face-to-face goodbyes. How has June matured in the realm of farewells?

23. Not much is mentioned about Jimmy's parents and upbringing, until Chapter 39. How do Jimmy's thoughts about his parents impact June?

24. How does June's explanation of how she wants the public to treat her (in Chapter 40) resonate with you? If you've suffered a loss, do you agree with her?

25. The momentous final chapter reveals a bit about June's living situation and her future. If there were a next chapter, what do you think would happen in it?

26. What do you think is in the letter June is sending to Paul at the end of the last chapter?

Snow Ice Cream Recipe

1 cup milk or cream
½ cup sugar
1 tsp. vanilla extract
8-10 cups fresh snow

Whisk ingredients together and enjoy immediately!
Add sprinkles or chocolate syrup if you wish.